D0097108

CODE NAME MOCKINGBIRD
A Paranormal Women's Fiction Novella

Copyright © 2022 Kristen Painter

Published in the United States of America

What does a retired vampire hunter do with the rest of her life?

That's a question Bess Walker-James is desperately trying to figure out. Having recently been made redundant, she holes up at her family home in Maine to do some serious thinking about what comes next.

Unfortunately, she has no idea.

Until her handsome next-door neighbor shows up. Turns out, Callum McCarthy needs more help than just finding his missing cat. Bess decides to assist him. What else has she got to do? But little does she know he's a lot more than he seems.

Of course, so is she…

Chapter
One

Everleigh Manor was eight thousand six hundred twenty-seven square feet. Needless to say, it was a lot of house. Nine bedrooms, six and a half bathrooms, plus a slew of other rooms that all added up to it being abundantly too much for one person.

Not that it was really meant for one person.

But Bess Walker-James had nowhere else to go now that she'd been made redundant. She rolled her eyes at that term. Was that supposed to make forced retirement sound better? Because it didn't.

Redundant. If the word had a throat, she'd punch it.

At least she had Everleigh to camp out in for a while. Because of the amount of travel her job had entailed, she'd never needed a permanent home. Now she did. And Everleigh Manor, as ridiculously big as it was, as filled with antiques and priceless objets d'art as it was, remained her best and easiest option. It was hers, after all.

Arms crossed, she stared out at the rocky coastline and the green, churning sea beyond the protruding bluff the house was built on. A massive deck sprawled to the left and right of the French doors, encompassing the entire back of the house so that the coast could be enjoyed from all the rooms that fronted it.

Without question, the house and property were beautiful, but today the whole thing, including the gray clouds that threatened snow, just reminded her of how foul her mood was at the moment. It was nearly 3 p.m., however. Soon the sun would go down and she wouldn't even have the coast to look at.

She'd face another bleak night thinking about what had just happened to her and trying to figure out what she was going to do with the rest of her life.

How dare ARROW, the Active & Ready Resistance Order of Warriors, force her to retire? So what if she was fifty-nine? That wasn't old for a woman like her. She was in perfect fighting form. Granted, her boss had offered her a desk job, but after almost forty years of fieldwork, did they really expect her to jump on *that?*

Not bloody likely.

If she'd wanted to sit at a desk all day, she would

have gone into admin when she'd first been recruited in college. She inhaled, tasting the hint of salt in the air, and as an onslaught of memories came at her, the sea beyond the property's borders blurred.

The old days had been something else. Rogue vampires had been everywhere. So had black magic witches. And rabid packs of werewolves, which, in all honesty, were probably still around. But back then, the world had been rife with paranormal creatures causing trouble. She smiled. She and her teammates had cleaned out so many nests that a lot of the baddies had been eliminated. A lot more had gone underground.

Way underground.

And then things had begun to change. Treaties had been enacted. Truces had been called. Harmony was the new supernatural buzz word. She rolled her eyes again. Sure, because humans were going to get on board with integrating monsters into their daily lives.

Whatever. Didn't mean there wasn't still a need for hunters like her. Or that there would stop being a need. Infestations cropped up all the time. Just last month there had been a plague of red demons in Uganda. Then there was that swarm of diseased pixies in Arizona that had shut down a multimillion-dollar health and wellness retreat.

Solo cases hadn't really declined, either. Just wait a minute and you'd hear about a new serial killer cropping up that was obviously a vampire gone rogue.

But those jobs always ended up being given to other hunters. *Younger* hunters.

Fifty-nine was *not* old. Not for a woman with her gifts and abilities. With her extraordinary bloodline. And ARROW knew that. Those lousy ageist creeps.

She pulled her cardigan tighter over her pajamas. From the kitchen, she heard the coffeepot sputter as it finished brewing. With a final glance at the world beyond the French doors, she turned and went to get a cup.

She filled an oversize mug with coffee to about an inch below the rim, then added three spoons of sugar and topped it off with salted caramel creamer. The smell wafted up, teasing her senses, but she already knew how good it was going to taste.

Sadly, a great cup of coffee did not an afternoon make.

Once again, she was faced with how to spend yet another day of doing nothing useful. Yesterday, she'd shifted into a goshawk and cruised the coast, but the wind had been brutal, and she'd gotten tired of fighting it. She supposed she could turn herself into a harbor seal and do some swimming.

Whatever the activity, she refused to sit in front of the television again all night, half-watching something inane while she scrolled her phone. And while she loved a good book, reading all evening wasn't exactly the most productive, either.

And she was used to being productive. That was the hardest thing about this stupid retirement. Not knowing what to do with herself. She wasn't the artsy-fartsy type that was about to take up loom-weaving or watercolor impressionism or pottery, although in Passat Cove, those pursuits would probably make her fit right in.

Although she could go wander around town for a bit. Maybe get familiar with the place. Grab a scoop or two of homemade ice cream, if Fat Mama's was still there. That much she remembered from her summers here as a kid.

She also knew that the community outside of the exclusive mansions that lined the coast was all about artsy-fartsy. She'd seen signs for the annual fall craft festival as she'd been driving in.

Just what she needed. Potholders made out of junior's middle-school T-shirts. Or maybe some reusable grocery bags crocheted from old lobster lines. No thank you.

She could get another job, but doing what? She'd spent her life dispatching supernatural pests.

Not much call for that in the human world. Yet. She sipped her coffee. Maybe that would change if the paranormal crowd really did push for integration. But that could be a long way off. And she needed something to do now.

Not because of the money. The retirement package she'd received from being made redundant had been generous enough, but money had never been the motivating factor. She came from money.

This stupidly enormous house was proof of that.

She took her coffee back to the living room and stood in front of the French doors again. She'd been coming to this house since she was a child, back when it had belonged to her great-great-grandfather, Herbert Walker-James, a shipping magnate who'd also been at the right place at the right time during the industrial revolution.

He'd chosen Passat Cove, Maine, as the place to build his summer home, along with a bunch of his almost equally as wealthy peers, and the rest, as they said, was history. Passat Cove became a bit of a haven for wealthy industrialists at the time, as evidenced by the enormous houses that dotted this part of the coastline.

Quite a few of them had changed hands over the years. One had even been turned into a small, exclusive resort. But not Everleigh Manor.

The house had traveled down through the family until it had ended up with her, the last direct descendant of the Walker-James line. And so here she was. The family trust paid the salaries of the housekeeper and the caretaker, a married couple by the names of Rosario and Luis who also lived on the property, but other than those folks, she was alone.

Or was she? Movement on the deck caught her eye. A cat. A big, fluffy, brown and black striped one with white feet and chin. A Maine coon maybe? He, or she, looked too well fed to be a stray.

That alone intrigued her. This time of year, most of the houses were empty. After all, these were summer homes, never really meant for year-round residence. Shocking that places this big were used so little, but that was the reality of it. Summers in Maine were spectacular, but in the late fall and winter, the state wasn't exactly the most hospitable place, as the weather outside was trying hard to prove.

She set her coffee on a side table and opened one

of the French doors. The cold wind whipped past her as she crouched down and held out her hand. "Here kitty, kitty."

Did he have a collar on? Seemed like it. A little hard to tell with all that fur. "Come on, you can't stay out here in this cold. Although you're probably warmer than I am with that coat you have on."

The cat sauntered over at a remarkably slow pace, but now that he was facing her, she could see he did have a collar on, and the collar had a tag.

He stopped just out of reach and sat down to stare at her.

"Seriously, my man, you're letting all the heat out. If you come inside, I'll give you a can of tuna while I call your owner to come get you."

There had to be tuna in the pantry. Before she'd arrived, she'd emailed Rosario and Luis to let them know she was coming so they didn't think there was an intruder in the house, and both had replied that they would prepare the house for her arrival. Rosario had also asked for a list of groceries.

Bess had given Rosario a small list of the essentials (her favorite brand of coffee, her all-important salted caramel creamer, some nice steaks, a good supply of baking potatoes, apples, and premium double chocolate ice cream) but then just asked

Rosario to stock the fridge and pantry with whatever else she thought the place needed.

Bess hadn't been in the right mindset to do more than that. She hadn't looked in the pantry since she'd arrived a few nights ago, either. The coffee and sugar had been waiting on the counter for her, the creamer in the fridge. To feed herself, she'd relied solely on the food in the fridge and a pizza she'd ordered in from Dom's Pies. But she assumed Rosario had stocked accordingly.

The sugar had definitely been purchased recently because if it had been sitting around for a while, it would have been hard as a rock.

Bess made a little noise at the cat, clicking her tongue. "Please, kitty cat. My coffee is getting cold. And you really shouldn't spend the night out here alone. There are hawks." Although he looked too big to carry off. "Don't you want tuna?"

The cat picked up a front paw, licked it twice, then smoothed it over his ear.

Bess let out a sigh. "All right, I'm done playing games." With the kind of speed only she could generate, she snapped forward, grabbed the cat by the scruff, and pulled him inside. As she did that, she closed the door with her foot and rocked back to sit on her backside.

But the cat jumped forward at the same time, and the momentum put her flat on the floor. The cat ended up on her chest, staring down at her with what might have been contempt for her kidnapping.

She shrugged from her prone position. "You left me no choice." She tipped her head to see his tag better. "Hello, Murphy."

On the back of the engraved metal rectangle was a phone number. Not a local number, but then with cell phones, who really had a local number anymore? The collar wasn't any ordinary old nylon one, either. It was brown coated canvas with a distinctive pattern that belonged exclusively to Louis Vuitton.

"You definitely live in the neighborhood, don't you, Murphy?"

He hopped off and sauntered toward the kitchen, apparently ready for her to make good on her promise of tuna.

She got up and went after him. "All right, hang on." Then to herself, "Let's hope Rosario thought tuna was a staple."

The pantry was the size of a small guest room. Bess flipped on the light and was immediately impressed. Rosario had apparently thought everything was a staple, from flour and more sugar to canned soup and veggies and everything in between, including lots of pasta in various shapes, jarred sauces, packaged cookies, cereal, syrup, a variety of pickled items, several kinds of rice, crackers, and condiments.

Plenty of canned meats, too. Smoked oysters, baby clams, salmon, and most thankfully, tuna. Three kinds. Bess picked the one that was packed in spring water, thinking the two that were packed in Italian olive oil might upset Murphy's system, and she didn't want to be responsible for that.

Or for upsetting one of her neighbors.

She took it back out to the kitchen. Murphy was up on the countertop, sniffing the potted herbs growing on the windowsill over the sink. Bess snorted. "You sure get comfy fast."

She pulled the tuna lid off, dumped it into a bone china bowl that bore the Walker-James monogram, and set it in front of him.

He wasted no time getting his face in the bowl.

While he did that, she twisted his collar around, pushing his thick fur out of the way, and read the number again. Her phone was in the bedroom, which felt like a mile away at the moment. She didn't really want to leave Murphy on his own either. He could get lost in this house pretty quick, and there was no litter box.

Wouldn't do to have him leaving naughty presents on the Oriental rug in the living room. Her mother had once told her it was insured for a hundred grand.

She grabbed the house phone and dialed, thankful that the landline was kept active in case of emergencies.

She got an answer on the third ring.

A man with a charming Irish lilt. "Hello?"

"Hi, you don't know me, but your cat just showed up on my back deck. Any chance you're missing one?"

"Murphy? I love my boy, but he can be a right bugger."

"That's the name on the collar."

"Thank you. He slipped out on me earlier. I don't even know how the door got open, but he's got the wanderlust, that one. Do ya mind hanging onto him until I can get there?"

"No problem. He seems hungry." Bess wasn't sure Murphy had stopped to breathe yet. "Do you mind if I give him some tuna?"

"That would be very kind of you, but I don't want to cause you any bother."

"It's no bother. I'm Bess, by the way."

"Nice to meet you, Bess. I'm Callum McCarthy.

Any chance you live on Dark Harbor Road, then?"

It took her a second to realize he'd asked her a question. She'd been lulled a bit by the dreamy sound of his voice. "Um, yes." What was wrong with her? He was probably half her age and married. Not that she was even remotely interested in any man at the moment. That was the last thing she needed. "I do. Does that mean we're neighbors then? Or you live nearby? I thought you might, although I wasn't sure how far a cat might roam."

"I live on Dark Harbor as well."

Despite the years that had passed since she'd been here last, something clicked in her head. "Did you say your last name was McCarthy?"

"That's right. Should I assume you know my house then?"

She laughed. Who didn't know the McCarthy estate? Built with bootlegging money, maintained with legitimate whiskey sales soon after, although now they made gin, too. "You should. I'm guessing you might know mine as well. Everleigh Manor?"

"I do."

If memory served, they were separated by four or five properties. "I'll be home all evening, so stop by anytime."

"Thank you. I'm in the village, actually, running a

few errands, so it might take me an hour or so. Is that all right? Do you mind keeping an eye on Murphy until then?"

"Not at all." She scratched the cat on the head. He was just about done eating. "Is this your cell phone?" Ugh. What a stupid question. Of course it was his cell phone. He'd just said he was in the village. That stupid accent was making her dumb.

"It is, which means I have your number. Call if anything changes. And thanks again."

"You're welcome. See you in a bit."

They hung up, and Bess looked at Murphy, who was now cleaning himself. "I hope you can be a good boy if I leave you alone because I wasn't expecting company and now that your father is coming to get you, I really need to shower."

CHAPTER
TWO

B ess had obviously planned to shower, just not quite so soon. Her plan, not that she'd really had one beyond the eventual shower, had been more about drinking several cups of coffee while contemplating the new wrinkle in her life and remaining braless in her cardigan and pajamas, which were just silk pants and a cotton tank top.

Now a man was on his way over here, and even if he wasn't here for longer than the five minutes it took to hand him his cat and make some neighborly small talk, she had too much pride to be seen looking like she was completely aimless.

Even if that was true.

She didn't want to start any rumors, either. Because while Everleigh Manor might be the perfect place to hide away and sort her life out, Passat Cove was a small town. *Small*. When the tourists went home, which had already pretty much happened, Passat Cove shrunk to about six thousand actual residents.

Winters were long and harsh, and if there was

anything townies liked to do to pass those brutal months, it was talk about the rest of the people who lived in Passat Cove. Especially those in the big houses along the coast.

Her great-grandmother had been the subject of many of those gossipy conversations, creating a notoriety that her grandmother and mother had worked tirelessly to defuse.

Bess didn't really want to unravel all that work and become known as the newest crazy heir to the Walker-James fortune.

She wanted less attention. Not more.

And so she showered and washed her hair and put some makeup on. She used the blow dryer under the sink to get the dampness out of her silver hair. She kept it long enough to braid or secure back into a ponytail. Short hair would have been easier in her line of work, but she'd never been a fan of her ears.

Even supernatural bounty hunters could be a little vain now and then. Not that what she was currently doing was rooted in vanity. More like self-preservation. She was just trying to make a decent first impression. She was going to be living here. And she wanted to stay under the radar as much as possible.

Then she got dressed in her most normal outfit.

In other words, not the black tactical pants, black T-shirt, boots, and leather jacket she most often wore for work. No weapons, amulets, or body armor, either.

Instead, she was in *a bra,* medium-wash jeans with a simple heather gray sweater, black leather loafers, and the strand of pearls and pearl studs she'd inherited from her mother ages ago. Another item that had been passed down over the years.

She only really wore them for dressy or serious occasions. She'd last worn them when she'd been called into ARROW headquarters.

When she thought she'd been about to get a promotion.

Idiots. *Redundant.* Whatever.

A quick once-over in the mirror and she was satisfied with what she saw. She'd aged well, but that was a gift of her bloodline. She turned the pearl strand around so that the diamond clasp was hidden in the back. She wasn't really the kind of woman who wore pearls so much as a dagger strapped to her thigh, but for the moment she was all about the right impression at the right time.

She turned the light off in her bathroom and went toward the hall.

For all she knew, Callum McCarthy might show

up with his wife and kids in tow. He'd never said he was out alone. And if they were coming here, the wife might angle for a tour of the place. Old money loved to see how other old money lived.

Which was fine. Bess had nothing to hide. Outside of the arsenal of personal weapons she'd stashed in the closet of her bedroom. She glanced back at the room as she walked into the hall. Impulsively, she pulled the door shut. She was going to keep it that way, too. And then there'd be no issue. Really, they didn't need to see that room. There were plenty of others in the house. Far more interesting rooms, too.

Like the one that housed her great-great-grandmother's collections of curiosities, including a range of memento-mori jewelry, criminal ephemera, occult objects, and skulls from various creatures.

The side of Bess's mouth hitched up in wry smile. Great-great-grandmama Mamie had been a strange old bird. But then, most of the women in this family had been, thanks to their gifts. Bess wished she could have known her.

She strode back into the kitchen to check on Murphy. He was sprawled out on the counter, his front leg outstretched to serve as a pillow for his massive head.

"Hello, Murph. Having a snooze?"

He let out a sigh, apparently bored with her attempts at conversation.

She nodded. "I completely understand. I'm a little out of practice when it comes to small talk."

Not much call for small talk when you were killing demons or setting snares for mangy were-wolves intent on harvesting a town's slow movers.

She leaned on the counter, struck by the fact that Murphy was the first non-ARROW company she'd entertained in … decades? Maybe longer.

Her best hope with the McCarthys was to get them in and out as quickly as possible so she didn't do or say something stupid. Then, once they were gone, she could go back to moping around and contemplating her next move in life.

What on earth was that going to be? Dodder around this house for the rest of her days? That sounded … fatally boring.

She wasn't cut out for that kind of life. She liked adventure and risk with a little danger thrown in. Just enough to keep the heart pumping and the blood circulating. That was the real fountain of youth right there.

There was no hobby or pastime that would give her the same satisfaction as ridding the world of some supernatural bad guy. Collecting things that creeped other people out had promise, for sure, but she liked making a real difference. Liked feeling that what she did meant something.

Maybe that was why she was struggling so much with being made redundant. Because ARROW had suddenly decided she wasn't worth keeping around.

All because of her age.

Honestly, it was a lawsuit waiting to happen. But pursuing such a thing would mean breaking the vow of secrecy she'd taken when she'd first been hired. A vow she'd sealed in blood and backed with her own life.

No matter how angry she might be, she wasn't stupid. ARROW would come after her. And she valued her life, even if it turned out to be sad and boring.

She supposed she could freelance, but there were a lot of pitfalls to consider when going out solo. And she wasn't in the mood for that much thinking or planning right now.

She scratched Murphy behind the ears, making him close his eyes and purr. She smiled. "Maybe I should get a cat, huh? Or two? I could see going in the crazy cat lady direction. I mean, in this house, I could easily have thirty or forty of your friends in here and no one would ever know."

The image that quickly filled her head made her laugh. "Although Rosario would probably quit."

Bess sighed. Getting a pet wasn't a bad idea, but it wasn't going to solve anything other than giving her a little non-human companionship, which was probably the kind she was best suited for anyway.

She dumped the remains of her now cold coffee and poured a new cup from the pot, fixing it just like she had the previous cup.

She was halfway through it when the doorbell's melodious six notes played throughout the house. The McCarthys were here. She glanced at Murphy. "Looks like I'm done cat-sitting. Don't go anywhere."

Leaving her cup behind, she walked to the door, peering through the leaded glass in the top half. A sleek metallic black Mercedes with windows tinted the same inky shade was parked on the curve of the drive. It looked brand new. She opened the door and did her best not to stare at the man in the black leather moto jacket across from her, but *Holy Hannah,* he was good looking.

Not only was Callum McCarthy alone, but he also wasn't *that* young. Gray dusted his temples, and lines bracketed his eyes and mouth. The kind of lines that made men seem somehow sexier and women like they needed better moisturizer.

He smiled at her, making those lines flex and his eyes twinkle. Something *odd* happened inside her, too. A reaction that could only be described as interest. "You must be Bess. I'm Cal McCarthy. I hope this is a good time."

She nodded, wordlessly, not done taking him all in. Then she remembered her manners. "Yes, this is fine, and I'm Bess. Nice to meet you, Cal."

Mother of pearl, handsome barely covered it.

His smile went from pleasant to amused. He shoved his hands into the pockets of his weathered black jeans, rippling the hem of his dark blue T-shirt. "You do still have Murphy, don't you?"

She blinked. "Oh, right, yes, sorry." She took a step back, getting out of the way so he could enter, a little embarrassed that he'd affected her that much.

He didn't move, however, just continued to smile at her. Then his nostrils flared and something dark flickered in his gaze. Something very much like hunger. He tilted his head slightly. "Aren't you going to invite me in?"

And that's when she knew.

Callum McCarthy was a vampire.

CHAPTER
THREE

She froze, struck with indecision. If she didn't let him in, he'd get suspicious. After all, she had his cat. And if she did, she'd be giving a vampire access to her home.

Neither of those sat well with her.

Then he laughed softly, shaking his head. "I see you know what I am."

"I …" She frowned, not quite sure she wanted to admit to that.

"It's okay." He shrugged. "You don't have to invite me in. You can just bring Murphy to me. I'll wait here. Or you can invite me in and then rescind the invite when I leave. But I promise, I'm not here to do you any harm."

She wasn't so sure about that.

He gave her a long, hard look, clearly picking up on her doubts. "I'd rather take you to dinner than make you my dinner."

A little shiver swept through her. Pleasure? Trepidation? She wasn't sure. Maybe both. "You're admitting to me what you are?"

His brows lifted. "Yes. I'm telling you I'm a vampire. That's what you were thinking."

Could he read minds? Some of the really old ones could.

"And no, I can't read minds. I just saw it on your face. That moment of recognition when I asked to be invited. It seems likely that you've had the opportunity to meet my kind before. Perhaps not the most neighborly of interactions either. I apologize if they were less than jovial."

She should have strapped on a few blades, just in case. But that ship had sailed. Still, there were plenty of knives in the kitchen. She nodded. "You're right. I have known a few vampires. None of them particularly pleasant."

Like the one in Hungary who'd drained half the nuns in a convent before Bess had been able to hunt him down and stake him.

She smiled. "Please, come in." Better to keep your enemies close. "Murphy's in the kitchen."

"Cheers." He wiped his boots on the mat before stepping inside. "Your perfume is lovely."

"Thanks." She wasn't wearing any. Another hallmark of her kind was how delicious they smelled to vampires. Something she'd used to her advantage for years as a hunter.

He took a look around. "This is a grand place, isn't it?"

"It is." His Irish burr was stupidly charming. So much so that she kept forgetting he was the potential enemy. "Although I had nothing to do with that. It's looked like this for a long time." She led the way to the kitchen, not completely happy with having him at her back. She glanced at him. "Isn't yours the same way?"

"Mostly. But I've been around long enough to have everything to do with how it looks, other than a few rooms which I've left as is. Sentiment and all that. You should come over and have a look."

"Really?"

"Sure, look, isn't that the neighborly thing to do? You show me yours; I show you mine?"

Despite her misgivings, she laughed as they walked into the kitchen. Murphy hadn't moved. "I didn't realize it was reciprocal." She gestured at the sleeping cat. "There he is, safe and sound."

"Murph, you rotten thing." Cal scooped him up and kissed the top of his head. "You had me worried sick, boyo." Still cradling the cat like a baby, he looked at Bess. "I'm too attached. I know that. But he's such good company. I love the silly bugger."

She smiled. It was hard not to like a man who

was softhearted toward his pet. Even if that man was a vampire. "He hasn't been any trouble. Ate a can of tuna, then passed out. Does he escape often?"

"Not often, but if he gets the chance, he'll take it. Which is still too much for my taste." He frowned at the cat, who was now kneading his enormous paws in the air under Cal's chin. "Please, let me take you to dinner to say thank you."

Bess crossed her arms and leaned on the counter. "It's not necessary. I didn't do it for any kind of reward."

"That's kind of you. But might you also be a bit worried what the townies might say? Two coasties out for a bite?" He grinned, and she could have sworn she saw a hint of fangs before they disappeared. "Or is it because of what I am? If that's the case, you can pick the restaurant. Most public place you can think of."

She lifted one shoulder in a noncommittal gesture. "I'm pretty busy getting settled in. I appreciate the offer, but I was just doing the neighborly thing."

His eyes narrowed. "Do I scare you then?"

"Ha!" The laugh came out like a bark, louder and more forcefully than she'd intended.

Murphy's eyes came open, and he bolted out of

Cal's arms, taking off like a shot toward the north wing of the house.

"Son of—" Cal lifted up his T-shirt to have a look at his stomach. Three long, parallel scratches ran across his midsection. Blood was rising to the surface.

Bess couldn't help but notice that the man had the most amazing abs. An actual six-pack. Not so unusual among vampires, granted, but impressive nonetheless. "I'm sorry. I didn't mean to scare him."

As she spoke, the red lines disappeared, healing right in front of her.

Cal dropped his T-shirt. "I know you didn't. Good to know I don't scare you either. But the bad news is Murphy is a world-class hider." He looked past her, in the direction the cat had gone. "I'm not sure we'd be able to find him if we wanted to. Which we do, I realize. Just saying, he won't come out until he's good and ready."

Bess sighed. That wasn't how this was supposed to go. "Maybe if I put some more food out?"

"He just had a can of tuna, yeah?"

"Yes."

Cal shook his head. "Then he'll be hunkered down for a while. Unless he needs to do his business. Then ..." He grimaced and let out a sigh. "I don't suppose you have a litter box in this house, do you?"

"Nope."

Cal closed his eyes for a moment and took a breath. Probably just another reflexive action, like the sigh, not because he needed air. "We should have a quick look for him, although I doubt we'll find him until he's ready to be found. After that, I'll run to the store and get one."

"We should definitely look." Bess felt bad. "Wait. He's not some kind of supernatural creature, too, is he?"

"No. Just an ordinary but very wily cat."

"Okay, we'll look. Then I'll go to the store with you. It's my fault he bolted."

"It's my fault he got out in the first place. Even though I swear I don't remember leaving a door open."

"Then we'll share the blame. But you can drive."

Half an hour later, they'd searched every inch where Murphy could be hiding. Thankfully, a lot of the rooms were closed off. Her bedroom included.

"I told you," Cal said. "He's a stubborn git. Time to go to the store."

"All right, I just need to get my purse and my jacket."

He nodded, a hint of a smile visible. "That's kind of you to go with me." He hooked his thumb toward the front of the house. "Meet you out front?"

She nodded. "Five minutes."

As he headed for the door, she stayed where she was until she heard him leave. Then she went to her bedroom for her purse. And to strap a dagger to her calf and slip another sheathed dagger under the waistband of her jeans.

Cal seemed nice enough and nonthreatening enough, but she'd spent too many years in the field and seen plenty of vampires who were the opposite of that to take chances.

As much as she wanted to throw on her field jacket, she didn't. Instead she opted for a navy wool blazer she found in the closet with a few other items. Her late mother's, maybe? Her things were still all throughout the house. The fabric smelled a little like mothballs, but so what? She didn't care what Cal—or anyone—thought.

She slipped the strap of her bag over her shoulder, a simple crossbody with enough room for a third dagger in a specially constructed hidden sheath on the back. It was the only ARROW-issued item she'd kept, and she had no intention of ditching it. Way too handy.

She checked herself in the mirror to be sure none of her weapons were visible, then went out to the front of the house.

She took one more look for Murphy on her way out. Nothing.

She locked the front door behind her and walked to Cal's car.

He was leaning against it, but as she approached, he straightened and opened the passenger door for her. "Any sign of him?"

She shook her head before getting in. "Not a whisker."

"Such a bugger." Cal shut the door and came around to the driver's side, sliding in behind the wheel. He started the car and went down the long drive to the main road.

Most of the homes along the coast, the big homes anyway, had very long drives with plenty of trees between them and the road. They offered a nice bit of privacy, even at this time of year, when the leaves were nearly gone.

He stopped to check for traffic before turning. "You're awfully calm for a woman with a cat loose in her antique-laden, multimillion-dollar, litter-box-free home."

She chuckled. "The house has survived worse. I

don't think Murphy having an accident will be what causes its demise. Although if he pees on that rug in the living room, you might hear from my grandmother's ghost about that one."

Cal grinned. "Feel free to give her my address. And if that does happen, I will pay for the cleaning."

She leaned back, watching him out of the corner of her eye so as not to be too conspicuous. He was handsome. Easygoing. Dressed in that casual and unshowy way of people who'd had money a long time, although she'd bet that nothing he had on had been purchased at Renys, Maine's own department store. Probably more like … wherever wealthy people who weren't supernatural hunters shopped.

He seemed pretty much like a typical Mainer with money in all regards. Maybe not as preppy as that type had been once upon a time, but he was also Irish, so he couldn't be expected to adopt the full Americana most in these parts favored.

No, there was nothing about him that sent up alarms.

Other than the part where he was a vampire.

CHAPTER
FOUR

Bess assessed her situation. She might be in a small, confined space with a vampire, but she had the upper hand. He needed to pay attention to the road. And she was well-trained and decently armed.

Emboldened, she decided to find out more about her neighbor. "How long have you been a vampire?" It wasn't generally something you could tell just by looking at a vamp, but he'd arrived at her house while it was still daylight, so she had her suspicions.

"All my life." He glanced at her before putting his eyes back on the road.

She wondered if he'd seen the reaction he'd been expecting. "So that's what kind you are ..."

His brows shot up. "You know a lot about vampires."

She frowned at herself. She'd slipped up. Revealed too much. What human knew there were different kinds of vampires? Not many, she imagined. And even though she'd already told him she'd encountered vamps before, she did her best to cover, shrugging it off. "I just heard that there are two kinds of vampires. Turned and born."

That wasn't true. There were three kinds. Turned, born, and resurrected. The last kind were the worst. Like a zombie combined with a vampire and extremely hard to kill.

He nodded as if he was taking that in. "There are actually three kinds, but that's not important. And yes, I'm one of those."

"Does it matter?" she asked. "What kind you are?" It did to her. Mostly because of how a vampire's origin affected their abilities. How hard it made them to kill. How powerful they might be. Or could become, given enough time.

Turned were the easiest to kill. Resurrected were much harder. Born were almost impossible because born vampires had a much stronger immunity to the sun as evidenced by Cal's being outside before dusk. Made them feel—and act—invincible.

She wasn't feeling quite as secure as she had been a few seconds ago, but thankfully they were on Main Street now and even though darkness was quickly descending, there were people on the streets. Passat Cove was well-lit, too, thanks to an endowment by her family years ago that provided money for quaint streetlamps.

Thank you, great grandpa Willard.

"It matters to most of my family," Cal answered. "They consider born vampires to be the aristocracy of our kind." He snorted. "Whatever bloody good that does."

She chose her words carefully. "I suppose in … vampire circles it means something. Around here? All that matters is your address."

He nodded. "True that."

Just the mention of Dark Harbor Road made most people's brows rise.

He pulled into the parking lot of the Hannaford's grocery store and found a spot. He turned the car off, then looked at her, one side of his mouth lifted in a half-smile. "Shall we go mingle with the commoners and give them a thrill?"

She snorted with amusement. "You're pretty funny for the undead."

The half-smile became a full. "Thanks."

They got out of the car and went in. The shop was busy, mostly with people looking for dinner on their way home from work. The pet aisle wasn't as crowded. Cal drove the carriage, pushing it along like he went shopping all the time.

Maybe he did. Bess would have thought he had staff for that. But maybe it was hard to get staff when you were a vampire. Although most humans wouldn't know unless he did something to reveal himself.

Which made her wonder what he was thinking about her. He had to question why she'd picked up on him being a vampire so quickly.

He came to a stop in front of the shelves that held the litter supplies. "Can you believe this? No boxes."

She snapped out of her reverie to pay attention. "What?"

He nodded at the shelf. The spot where the plastic litter trays should have been was empty. "Not a one. Low on litter too." He grabbed a jug and put it in the cart.

She got her phone out and did a quick search. "There's a place called Pet Pals in this shopping center."

"That's right," he said. "We should have just gone there. Looks like that's where we're headed now anyway." He put the litter jug back on the shelf. "Better to support a local shop anyway, don't you think?"

She tucked her phone away. "I'm all for that."

He put his hands back on the carriage handle. "Need anything since we're in here?"

Bess thought about the abundantly stocked

pantry she'd seen earlier. "No, I'm good. Rosario keeps the house well supplied."

"Rosario?"

"The housekeeper."

"Ah." The familiar amused twinkle returned to his gaze. "Well, then, your ladyship, shall we move on to the pet store?"

She gave him a good-natured but stern look. "Like you don't have a housekeeper?"

"Nah, I do. But I like taking the Mick out of ya."

She smiled and shook her head. "Keep it up and you're going to owe me some ice cream."

"That sounds grand, actually. Maybe after we get the kit for Murphy? I hear that Captain Scoops is good."

Bess made a face as they walked to the front of the store. "Captain Scoops is for tourists. You ought to know that. Fat Mama's is where it's at."

He slid the carriage back in line with the rest of them. "I don't go out much. But I'm game. Fat Mama's it is then."

They walked down to Pet Pals since it was just a few stores away. It wasn't as large as one of the big box pet stores, but they had more than enough to offer.

Cal started for the cat section, but Bess stopped

to look through the window into the adoption room. Two little black cats, not kittens but still fairly young judging by their size, were wrestling around and playing. They were very cute. She smiled watching them.

Cal appeared beside her. "Brothers. Four months old."

She looked at him. "How do you know?"

He tapped the info sheet that hung from the window in a plastic sleeve. "Says so right here. Along with their names. Chip and Dip."

She frowned. "Those are horrible names."

"I'm sure whoever adopts them will come up with something better."

She peered in the window again. One of them was licking the other one on the head. "They are pretty cute."

"Maybe you should take them home. You are about to get a litter box. Odd to have such a thing without a cat to go with it."

She slanted her eyes at him. "I have a cat to go with it. Yours."

"Sure, but he'll be coming home with me as soon as I can get my hands on him."

"I'll think about it. Let's get what we need."

"Right-o, cracking on." He picked out the largest

litter box they had, which seemed like overkill, but then Murphy was a big cat—next, a jug of litter and a few cans of cat food. Then they headed to the register, where he whipped out a black credit card and paid.

He carried the goods to the car as well, putting them in the trunk and then seeing to her car door again.

"You don't have to do that, you know."

"Do what?" He leaned on the open door as she got in. "Be a gentleman? Are you trying to get my ma after me?"

She just pursed her lips and said nothing, letting him close the door. Why was he being so friendly, though? Her life's experience might be making her a little paranoid, but his attentions didn't seem unhealthy, all things considered. She just couldn't stop herself from being cautious. Especially when it came to the intentions of a vampire.

He got behind the wheel. "All right, where's this Fat Mother's?"

"Fat Mama's. And it's just down the street, if my memory serves. Half a mile maybe?"

Mile and a half, as it turned out, but Cal didn't say anything. Just parked in the gravel lot and got out.

She did the same, smiling at the old building. It was just as she remembered it. She hoped the ice cream was still as good and still homemade.

"So," Cal said. "What do you recommend?"

"Whatever your favorite flavor is. It's all fantastic. And we'd better get in line." Despite the cool evening, a handful of other folks had thought ice cream was a good idea too. Maybe trying to get one last scoop in before the place closed for the winter.

She looked at him. "What is your favorite flavor?"

He shrugged as they started to walk to the end of the line. "I don't know."

She made a face. "You don't know what your favorite flavor of ice cream is?"

"I don't eat it very often. I'm sure I'll see something on the board that appeals."

Her gaze shifted to the selections. There was a lot to choose from. "There." She pointed at one near the bottom. "That one seems made for you. Chocolate Guinness."

He gave her an amused smile. "No self-respecting Irishman would sully the good name of Guinness by indulging in such a thing. I'm going to have the butterscotch blondie. What are you having?"

She studied the offerings. "There's almost too much to choose from, isn't there? When I was a kid,

I used to get cookie dough. I want something different tonight."

She checked the flavors of the day, which were on a separate sandwich board. "That's it, right there. Caramel bourbon pecan."

His brows bent. "That does sound good."

"I'll let you have a … taste." She'd almost said bite, then reconsidered.

The line moved along and pretty soon they were finding their way to a picnic table, cups of ice cream in hand.

Cal chose the one farthest away, giving them some space from all the other patrons. She was glad about that. She'd decided while waiting in line that she needed to find out what was really going on.

She'd never known a vampire to befriend a human without some intention. Not always good, either. Sure, it was possible he was just lonely, but then again … she wasn't really buying that.

She slid her cup toward him. "Get your spoon in there before I decide it's too good to share."

"All right. You want to try mine?"

She hesitated. "Sure." Then took a little bit on her spoon.

It was good. Sweet and buttery, but with just the right hint of salt and little chunks of blondie. Very smooth, too, with a slight smokiness at the end. More sophisticated than she'd imagined. She was almost bothered she hadn't gotten it herself, but she wasn't going to admit that to him.

She went back to her own flavor, which was delicious, and, braced with the boldness of sugar in her veins, dug into the matter at hand. "Why exactly are you being so nice to me?"

CHAPTER

FIVE

He frowned with the spoon still in his mouth. He pulled it out and swallowed the bite he'd just taken. "Do you think I shouldn't be nice to you? You rescued my cat, after all."

"I don't know about rescued. Your cat was on my deck. He could have just as easily showed up back at your house if I hadn't dragged him in."

"Possibly. But Murphy relies more on his looks than his brains, if you get my meaning."

"I do. And you're changing the subject."

Cal shook his head. "Are most people not nice to you? I really don't understand what you're driving at."

She leaned in, lowering her voice. "It took you all of two minutes after meeting me to admit what you are. You do that with every human you meet?"

His mouth thinned to a hard line for a moment. "Just the ones that figure out what I am as quickly as you did. Should I have lied?"

She was glad he hadn't. Would have made things very awkward. "No. But vampires generally do everything they can to avoid being detected. It's just odd."

He looked her square in the eyes, like he was challenging her to tell the truth as well. "You have a lot of experience with vampires, do you?"

She stared right back, unfazed by his directness. Maybe telling the truth wasn't such a bad idea. "I used to. Not anymore."

He held her gaze a moment longer, then went back to his ice cream. "I know."

He knew? A chill went through her that had nothing to do with what she was eating. Maybe she hadn't heard him right. "What did you say?"

He sighed, stuck his spoon into his ice cream, and stared toward the road. "I didn't want to do it like this."

"Do what?"

He looked at her again and in a soft voice said, "I know who you are."

She didn't want to read anything into that, but it wasn't the kind of statement she could just ignore without further information. "What do you mean?"

"You know what I mean, *Mockingbird.*"

She went completely still. No one outside of ARROW knew her by that name. Or should know that name. *No one.* And yet, her vampire neighbor that she'd just met somehow did. She stared at him, unable to put what she was thinking and feeling into words. Then one came to her. "How?"

He shrugged one shoulder, like the knowledge of her secret life was something he'd just randomly picked up. No big deal. "A friend knew about my particular situation and knew about you as well and suggested I reach out to you. I didn't think going to your door and introducing myself was going to work, so—"

"So you sent your cat over to my house to pretend to be lost?"

His face screwed up into the most curious expression. "If you think I'm capable of training Murphy to do anything, you definitely don't know a lot about cats. I promise you, that was an accident."

"Then what?"

"I was going to try to run into you accidentally in town. Something like that. But you never leave your house."

"You've been watching me?"

He rolled his eyes. "Not you. But I have motion-sensitive cameras at the front of my driveway, and I've been keeping an eye out for your car."

She sat back, shaking her head. "Why, though?

What do you need me for? You said something about your situation?"

He glanced at the road again. "I need someone with your level of expertise in … dispatching threats."

Her brows lifted. If he thought she was some kind of killer for hire that was going to take out his enemies, he couldn't be more wrong. "Listen, I don't subcontract. What I did for ARROW was very specific and all governed by the rules and regulations they set up. I'm not looking to clean up your competition, if you get *my* meaning."

He frowned. "I'm not asking you to clean up anything. I'm asking you to protect me."

She hesitated. "From what?"

"From whoever's trying to kill me."

That gave her a moment of pause. "Someone's trying to kill you?"

He nodded slowly. "Yes, and I'm not sure who. Six months ago, a threatening letter was left in my mailbox telling me to leave Passat Cove or I'd be here, six feet under, permanently. I ignored it. Seemed like the logical thing to do."

"It's one way to go." She took another bite of ice cream. "Is that it?"

He shook his head. "A month later, another letter

with the same message. Leave or forfeit my life. A few weeks after that, my brakes were cut, resulting in a serious accident that wrecked my car. Twice I was shot at while on my own property. At least one was a silver bullet because I dug it out of the tree it ended up in."

"Not to make light of the situation, but none of those things would have killed you. Okay, the silver bullet, maybe, if it was a clean shot through the heart at the precise angle, but—"

"And there's the Mockingbird I've heard so much about. Clinically detached."

She glared at him. "I'm not detached. I'm just very good at assessing a situation. Your life may have been threatened but not in a serious way."

He stabbed his spoon into his ice cream, which had begun to soften even in the chilly air. "My exterior security lights were replaced with UV bulbs. A gift basket was sent to my house. Wine and cheese. Both were laced with laudanum."

She considered this new information. "Okay, those are a little more deadly, but …" A couple walked past on the way to their car. She waited until they were in and had their doors shut. "But it sounds to me like whoever this person is, they don't know their vampires very well. Born vamps are extremely hard to kill."

"See?" He gestured at her. "You're already making progress."

She stared skyward and shook her head. "Cal, anyone could figure that out."

"Not anyone. I hadn't actually considered it myself until you just mentioned it."

"Really?"

He shrugged, watching the street. "I've been a little preoccupied trying not to die."

He genuinely seemed upset. She felt for him. "You're not comfortable being out, are you?"

He shook his head without looking at her. "Not so much, no."

"Then let's go back to my place and see if we can get Murphy, then you can go home."

He nodded. "Sounds grand." But he didn't move. Just kept his eyes on the road. "When I found the door open, then couldn't find him right away, I thought the worst. I'm so glad he ended up with you."

"You think whoever this is might hurt Murphy?"

He looked at her and shrugged. "I have no idea. But what's to stop them?"

She didn't like that. There was no telling what

Cal had done to make whatever enemies he had. But Murphy? He was the innocent here.

"Will you help me?" Cal asked. "I can pay whatever price you want."

"Who was the person at ARROW that told you about me?"

He answered with a little smile. "I can't tell you that. Would be a breach of trust."

"It's already a breach of trust that someone gave you my information." But she respected his refusal to snitch on a friend all the same. That felt like more loyalty than ARROW had recently shown her.

"So will you do it?"

She took one last bite of ice cream, letting it melt over her tongue while she thought. She was extraordinarily bored. And Cal was, so far, not the worst person she'd spent time with. She'd hate to find out something bad had happened to him that she could have prevented.

And then there was Murphy. She tapped her spoon on the side of the cup like she was thinking. "I am very expensive."

"And very worth it, I'm sure."

"You have to do what I say. You can't argue with me because you think you know best."

He was smiling now. Like this was amusing him. "I wouldn't dream of it."

She scanned the little groups of people around them. Could one of them be Cal's tormenter? She didn't catch a single one of them suddenly looking away or acting like they were trying hard not to be noticed.

But someone was clearly after him. She needed to find out why. But better to do that in a more secure location.

"You still haven't said yes, you know."

"I'll do it." A quiver of excitement zipped through her. It was good to be on mission again, even if it wasn't the kind of thing she was used to.

"Thank you."

"Don't thank me yet." She took a breath, then stood up, spoon and cup in hand to be thrown away. "We have a lot of work to do."

CHAPTER
SIX

She waited until they were back at her house before she asked any more important questions. His car could be bugged, for all she knew, and until she had a chance to search the vehicle's interior, she wasn't going to take the risk of being overheard. She'd typed out a note on her phone explaining that and shown it to him so that he'd keep quiet as well.

Once inside, however, she was ready to get her questions answered. "Okay, think hard. Who would want you out of Passat Cove so much that they'd threaten you with death? And why?"

"No one that I can think of. And I haven't a clue."

He had the litter jug in one hand and the box in the other, so she shut the door behind him before taking off her blazer. "Come on, that's a cop-out. No one is liked by everyone. Especially not a vampire."

"You didn't ask who didn't like me. You pretty much asked who might want to kill me. Those seemed like very different things." He looked past her. "Murphy? You around, boyo? Come out, pet."

No response from the cat, although Bess wasn't sure Cal had really been expecting one.

She went back to her line of questioning. "I'm not sure they are different. Depends on the person. So who doesn't like you? Start with whoever likes you the least."

Cal lifted the jug and box. "Shouldn't we set these up?"

"Oh, right. Guest bathroom is probably a good spot. It's sort of in the middle of the north wing. If that's where he still is. Come on, I'll show you." She led him down the hall after he'd hung his jacket on the coat stand by the door. "So? Who likes you least?"

"Probably Saraphina."

"And that is?"

With a little bitterness in his voice, he answered, "My ex-wife."

Bess glanced at him, brows raised. "Bad breakup? Bitter divorce?"

"Yes. And then some. I think she expected to get a good chunk of my money, but that didn't happen because I was able to prove she'd cheated on me."

Bess, looking straight ahead again, made a face. Who on earth would cheat on Cal? The man was hot. Sure, he was also a vampire, but Bess could appreciate male beauty of any variety when it was right in front of her.

Secondly, what kind of idiot would fool around with a vampire's wife? "Seems like a pretty good bet that she's not a Callum McCarthy fan. She could be behind your troubles, but would she care enough to go to the effort? Not sure. And how would she benefit from you leaving Passat Cove? Does she live here?"

"Not since the divorce. She moved to Las Vegas with her current boyfriend. He owns a casino and hotel."

"Was that the last guy she was cheating with? I have to admit, I'm curious about who was brave or stupid enough to cheat with a vampire's wife. If you don't mind me asking."

A long sigh came out of him. "I think she met him after the divorce was finalized. As for who she was cheating with, there were … several. I only know who one of them was, and he's back in France. A turned vamp by the name of LeMieux."

"Ah. I see." A turned vamp would know better than to come after a born vamp. Still, sleeping with one's wife? Not a very bright move. For him or the wife. "Your ex-wife sounds like a bit of a …"

"Player? Yeah."

"I was going to say floozy, but that too." She stopped at the guest bathroom and opened the door. "Here you go."

Cal got the box set up in the middle of the floor. "Sorry to tell you, but if this gets used, there will be litter on your floor. Murphy's a digger."

"It's fine. It's only temporary."

"True. But you're still going to have litter to clean up."

Couldn't be helped, as far as Bess could see. "I'll give Rosario a little extra if it's that big of a mess."

"Let me know and I'll chip in."

"You're already paying me. It's fine." She glanced down the hall to where the game room, library and theater were. "We should do another sweep of the house, don't you think? Call for him and all that?"

Cal nodded. "We should put some food out too. That's why I picked up a few cans."

"Good idea. Let's get through this section of the house, then head back to the kitchen and I'll get you a bowl."

They searched for Murphy, calling for him and making *psp psp psp* sounds, but there was still no sign of him by the time they'd returned to the kitchen.

"Unbelievable," Cal muttered. "Not even a meow."

Bess got another bone china bowl from the cabinet. "I'm sure he's just freaked out. New house, new smells. He'll peek his head out soon, don't you think?"

"No." Cal looked disgusted. "He could hide away for days. You don't know that cat. He's a right eejit when he wants to be."

Bess handed Cal the bowl and kept her comments about where Murphy might have picked up such a trait to herself. "Well, maybe the food will do the trick."

"Maybe."

"Even if it doesn't work right away, we have a lot left to talk about, anyway. I need as much information as you can give me. And you're probably safer here than at your own house, so unless you need to get back for something, you might as well stay. Murphy's probably more likely to come out if you're around, too."

He looked up at her. "Are you saying I should spend the night?"

She hadn't considered that. But it probably was the safest thing. For him. "Do you feel that you're in danger at your own home?"

His gaze seemed to go right through her. "Hard

to say until we know who's after me."

Was she going to regret this? She hoped not. "Then maybe you should stay here. I would like to go over to your house and have a look around. See the letters you were sent. But we can do that later. Assuming you keep late-night hours like I do."

"I do. Mind if I make another pot of coffee then?"

"Go right ahead." She gestured over her shoulder. "I'm going to grab my laptop so I can start a file and take notes. Be right back."

"No rush," he said.

Except that she had a vampire in her house. One she'd just invited to live in said house for who knew how long? She had to figure out who was threatening him and fast.

But first, she needed to decide what guest room to put him in. She'd like to put him in the north wing, as far away as possible, but logistically, that wasn't a smart move. If he was being watched, which seemed likely, there was every possibility his tormentor knew he was here.

Which meant they could try something at the first available chance. Probably when the house went dark and it could be assumed she and Cal had gone to bed.

The smart move would be to put him nearby. Smart from a mission standpoint.

Not so smart from any other.

Because try as she might to deny it, she was attracted to him. To a vampire. A thought that should have revolted her. But he was a nice guy. And a good conversationalist. An animal lover.

And then there was the elephant in the room. The fact that he'd given her a new purpose when she'd felt like that might never happen again. That purpose would end when she figured out who was threatening him, but it was enough to remind her that she was more than the woman who'd been made redundant by ARROW.

She was still Mockingbird. Still very capable of taking down supernatural villains. Something she was about to prove.

She walked toward her bedroom. Apparently, she'd left the door open the last time she'd left it. She flipped on the light.

Murphy was curled up on her bed, fast asleep. She grinned. "You are a bugger."

She grabbed her laptop, then hoisted Murphy over her shoulder with her other arm. "Ooph." He wasn't light, that was for sure.

He pushed his head against hers with surprising

strength, purring in her ear. She couldn't stop smiling. It was very sweet and certainly not something she was used to, but she could see the appeal of having a pet. Maybe those two black kittens weren't such a bad idea. "Come on, you big flirt. Your father will be happy to see you."

She walked into the kitchen and found Cal behind the refrigerator door. "Hungry?"

"Getting there. How about you?"

"A little. Even though we just had ice cream. I could go for something a little more substantial."

"Grand, 'cause I think I've got the makings of a fine meal right here, depending on what else I can rummage up in the pantry."

She was still grinning. "Is there enough for three?"

"What's that now?" He was still behind the door, digging around for something.

"Just saying we'll need to set an extra place."

Cal peeked out from behind the door, his hands filled with selections from the fridge. His mouth came open as he grinned. "Murph, you ole devil. On herself's bed, were you?"

"He was. Now come get him. He weighs more than my computer."

Cal dropped his groceries on the counter, then

lifted Murphy off her shoulder, taking a moment to detangle the cat from her hair. In the process, he brushed a few strands back over her shoulder, his fingers grazing the side of her neck and tripping sensations through her that she had no business feeling.

He held the cat up. "Try to be a good boy, now, will ya?" Then he put Murphy down by the food and water bowls on the floor.

"We should probably move the litter box into your bathroom now," Bess said.

Cal nodded as he started sorting through the food he'd gotten. "Good idea. What room do you want me in?"

She almost didn't answer. "I'm going to put you in the south wing. Near me. Just in case anything happens."

He grinned in a way that implied all sorts of things. "So you can protect me?"

"No, you're a big vampire, and you can protect yourself." She grinned right back at him. "I want you close so I can catch whoever's doing this and get you back to your own home."

He put his hand to his heart. "You wound me, Bess. I thought we were gettin' to be friends."

Her smile went nowhere. "We are, I suppose."

He snorted. "That must feel odd to you, eh? After a lifetime of turning my kind to ash."

That got rid of her smile. "They weren't your kind. They were killers. That's not who you are, is it?"

He shook his head, instantly serious. "Not by a long shot, love."

CHAPTER
SEVEN

For dinner, Cal made a wonderful version of pasta carbonara with eggs, bacon, and plenty of Parmesan, black pepper, and the surprising but delicious addition of a touch of lemon. Bess contributed a bottle of red wine, a Syrah that seemed like an interesting pairing.

They ate at the kitchen counter, sitting side by side, watching through the windows as darkness settled in around them.

"Franco Marr," Cal said as he twirled the few remaining spaghetti noodles around his fork.

The rich meal had lulled Bess into a state of contentment she'd not felt since getting axed. "Who's that?"

"Someone else who doesn't like me. A competitor in the spirits business. Claims McCarthy's gin uses the same formula as his family's secret recipe, which is rubbish. We don't. If anything, he'd like to be using ours. See, my great-great-nan created our gin recipe. And Moira was known for her recipes. Wasn't as if coming up with something like that was out of the ordinary for her."

"Does he live in the area? Or have a house here?"

"Family estate, toward the north end of Dark Harbor Road."

The north end had very nice houses but nothing like the estates on the south end, where she and Cal were. Bess sipped her wine. "Spirits are big business, aren't they?"

He nodded. "Massive."

"Enough money to make a man want to do you harm?"

"To get his hands on that recipe? More than enough."

Bess thought on that a little more. "Is he human?"

"Not altogether. There's a bit of the fae in him. Gives him keen senses, good speed, and the ability to vanish at will."

Bess swirled the last measure of Syrah in her glass. "Sounds about right for my experience with the fae." She drained the wine, then put her glass down and twisted her chair to face Cal. "I also know those with fae blood in them tend toward the devious side."

He snorted. "Oh, that's Franco Marr, all right."

"Liars, cheaters, thieves, grifters. Always trying to get something over on someone. And they succeed quite often. Has he ever tried to get money out of you to make the matter go away?"

Cal's brows bent. "As a matter of fact, he has. You do know your fae, don't you?"

"I know all supernaturals. It was my job for forty years. My life depended on how much I knew."

Appreciation shown in his gaze. "Did I mention that I find intelligence extremely sexy?"

She grinned, the wine making it impossible not to respond. "No, but—"

He pressed his mouth to hers, ending whatever she'd been about to say. She couldn't remember. His wine-flavored kiss had erased every thought in her head except for thinking about what he was doing and how long he was going to do it and how had her fingers ended up in his hair?

She snatched her hand away, then he pulled back a few inches.

Far enough to see her through his half-lidded gaze. "You are extraordinarily sexy, Bess. And you taste like honey. I don't know how that's possible."

He clearly didn't know what she was. Of course, he hadn't asked, and she hadn't volunteered that info so …

He sighed and moved back a little farther. "And I am a right fool. I shouldn't have kissed you. I'm not sorry I did, but I can at least acknowledge I shouldn't have done it. I'm not sure what got into me, but I was helpless to resist your charms."

He thought she had irresistible charms? Maybe it was the wine again, but she let out a soft laugh. "It didn't bother me." Surprisingly the truth. "Probably should have, but it didn't."

He started to lean in again.

She put her hand on his chest. "But I also don't think you should do it again. Not while I'm technically working for you."

And not until she could wrap her head around being kissed by a vampire. What an odd turn her life had taken.

He nodded. "Right. Shouldn't muddy the waters, as they say."

She was about to agree with him when a loud crash and the sound of glass breaking came from the front of the house.

The effects of the wine vanished as she jumped off her chair. Cal did the same, but she pointed at him. "Stay behind me."

To his credit, he did.

She approached the front of the house with

caution. One of the large picture windows in the formal sitting room was shattered, and a brick sat in the middle of the floor, surrounded by shards of glass. Wind blew the curtains into the room in long billows.

Butcher's twine secured a piece of paper to the brick.

"Just grand," Cal muttered. He sighed in disgust. "I'll pay for the damage."

"Don't touch anything until I get back," Bess said.

"Get back? Where are you going?"

"Outside to see if there's a trace of who threw that." Before he could argue, she turned and went the long way around to the front door so she could avoid the glass.

But he came with her. "What if they're still out there?"

"I'll handle it." She pulled her wool blazer back on. "But they aren't. Trust me, they're long gone." Actually, she was hoping they'd just retreated to the perimeter of the property to watch things unfold.

Cal put his hand on her arm. "Please let me come with you."

She glared up at him. "You hired me to do this, so let me do it." She gently took his hand off. "Just because you kissed me didn't suddenly make me vulnerable."

He frowned. "Right. Sorry. I keep thinking of you as human."

"Well, I'm not. So get that idea out of your head."

CHAPTER
EIGHT

The evening was moonless, and clouds covered the stars, but thanks to the landscape lighting, there was plenty of light to see by. Bess had pretty good vision, too. Maybe better than vampire or werewolf eyesight. Maybe not. Hard to say since there had never been a comparison done as far as she knew.

The ground was fairly solid in the cold weather, but they'd yet to get a hard freeze, so the dirt was soft enough to hold a footprint. In addition, Luis did a great job of maintaining the property, and the leaves on the yard had recently been raked. All of that meant it was pretty easy to see where feet had bent the grass or walked through dirt recently.

Someone had probably coasted down the drive, lights and engine off, since neither she nor Cal had picked up on the car's approach, then they'd run through one of the flower beds and about halfway across the yard to pitch that brick through her window.

She couldn't wait to read that note.

After investigating the flower bed and yard, she went back to the driveway and jogged to the end where it met the road. She slowed near the tree line, looking in both directions to see if there was a parked car anywhere around.

Nothing. Whoever had broken her window hadn't waited around. She looked at the woods beside her. Not in a vehicle, anyway.

She jogged back to the house to have a look at the note. She went straight to the sitting room.

Cal joined her. "Find anything?"

"Evidence of our visitor but nothing actionable." She picked her way through the glass to grab the brick. "This is so old-school."

"Brick through the window, you mean?"

"Yes." She hefted it in her hand. "Let's look at it in the kitchen."

He hesitated, still staring at the glass all over the floor. "What about this glass, though? And you can't leave that window like that. Murphy might do another runner. Or get cut if he were to come in here."

Her main thoughts were about the note and whoever was behind this, but he was right. "We'll shut the sitting-room doors for now."

"You have anything I could board that window

up with?"

She chewed at the edge of her bottom lip as she thought. "I have no idea. There's a workshop at the end of the detached garage, but that's Luis's domain. He keeps the riding mower and all the other yard tools in there. He might have some wood, but I'll just text him in a minute. I'd rather you not be out there when someone's trying to get to you."

"I can move pretty fast when I need to, you know."

She kept walking toward the kitchen. "I'm sure you can, but Luis will come fix it. That's why we have him, for general maintenance *and* emergencies. This qualifies as the latter."

Cal followed. "All right. But I want to pay for the replacement window."

"Fine with me." She put the brick on the counter, grabbed a knife from the block, and sliced the string. "Does this look like the same kind of paper your letters came on?"

"Could be. Seems like it."

She unfolded the paper.

Your new girlfriend can't save you. Get out while you still can.

"That was clearly meant for me," Cal said. "But I don't like that they've brought you into this."

"Same handwriting?" Bess asked. It didn't bother her at all that the note mentioned her. In fact, it confirmed that whoever was after Cal was absolutely watching him.

"Definitely."

Bess held the paper up, looking for a watermark. The ink was thick and black. She sniffed it. "Sharpie."

She put the note back on the counter. "I need to go have a look at your car. You can come with me this time, if you want." Only because she felt pretty certain whoever had thrown the brick had bolted.

"Yeah? All right."

"Grab your keys."

On the way out, she texted Luis about the window, asking him to come over as soon as he could unless he was in the middle of something. He and Rosario lived in the apartment over the detached four-car garage, so it wasn't like he had a long way to go. Wasn't really that late either. Just a little after nine.

He responded as they reached Cal's Mercedes, letting Bess know he'd be over in ten minutes.

Cal hit the button to unlock the car. "Just tell me what you need me to do."

"Hold this." Phone still in hand, she pulled off her

wool blazer and gave it to him. Then she got down on the ground and wriggled underneath the car, where very little of the landscape lighting could penetrate.

She turned on her phone's flashlight and started at one end of the car, scanning carefully.

"What are you looking for?" Cal asked.

"Tracking device." She knew where she'd put one. Not in a wheel well. Far too obvious. She favored placement behind the bottom of a door frame. That required a stronger than usual magnet, something of the rare earth variety, but tucking a tracker in like that meant it almost never got found. At least not without serious looking.

So was Cal's tormentor clever? Or not?

Bess smiled as her flashlight found something that didn't belong. "Not," she whispered.

She wrenched the small magnetic box free of the wheel well, then wriggled out and held it up. "Unless you keep a spare key under your car, here's part of how you're being watched."

"For real?"

She put her phone in her pocket, the pried off the box's cover. "Yep. GPS tracker."

She grinned at Cal. "Now let's go see if we can figure out where this little baby reports to."

"You can do that?"

She didn't want to overpromise. She was counting on not being locked out of the ARROW systems yet and having access to their database. "Maybe."

They headed back in.

"Thank you for finding that," Cal said. "Clearly, I was too thick to even think of looking."

Bess shrugged. "Civilians think differently than field agents. Not that I am one anymore, but I was one long enough. Old habits don't just disappear overnight."

"Color me impressed. Once again." He opened the front door for her.

She went to her laptop on the kitchen counter and fired it up.

"I'll clean up while you do that," Cal said. He gathered the dirty dishes and took them to the sink.

She glanced over as her computer came to life. "You cook and do dishes? Now it's my turn to be impressed."

He laughed. "I am a man of many talents."

"Good to know." She accessed the ARROW portal, then logged in.

Access denied.

Bess let out a muted curse. They'd already

deleted her from the system. "So much for that."

"Problem?" Cal asked.

"I won't be able to trace the tracker. It's fine." There was still plenty for her to do. She opened a new document and started typing in all the details she'd gathered so far. About a page and a half in, Luis arrived to fix the window. She showed him the sitting room, gave him a brief explanation of what happened, then went back to the kitchen.

But she didn't go back to the computer. She had more questions for Cal to answer. "Who has the most to gain from you leaving Passat Cove?"

He was drying the big pot he'd cooked the spaghetti in. Rosario was going to love him. "No one I can think of. And that's not a cop-out. That's the truth. The estate is mine, free and clear. I'm the oldest of my family."

"But that means whoever's next in line would inherit the property if you were gone. As in dead. Because if you just moved out, that wouldn't get them anywhere."

"You're talking about my younger brother, Dermot." Cal put the pot aside and shook his head. "I assure you, Dermot is happily ensconced in the family operations back in Ireland. He has no desire to live here, nor does his wife or their two boys."

So Cal thought. But could he really know that for sure? "How many brothers and sisters do you have?"

"After Dermot, there's Nora, then Siobhan. Four of us altogether."

"What other family members do you have?"

"My mum and my uncle Seamus. My late father's brother. He's got kids as well. They all work in the family business in Ireland, too. Except for my cousin Jamie. Good lad. He works here in the States, although he travels around visiting our big distributors, so I don't see him often. Although I do talk to him on the phone a fair bit."

"All vampires, I assume?"

"Yes."

"Any of them have designs on taking over the estate? Or even seem like they might?"

Cal narrowed his gaze. "Not so much that I could say."

"They've all been to the estate?"

He nodded. "Sure. Jamie lived there with me when he first moved over. But he's got a penthouse in Chicago now. Not that he's ever home."

She sighed in frustration. This was getting them nowhere. And she had the strangest feeling that time was running out.

CHAPTER
NINE

With Luis boarding up the damage and the tracker no longer on Cal's car, Bess felt like the time was right to go to Cal's house. It was probably being watched as well, but that was a chance they had to take.

She wanted to see those other letters and have a look around for herself. Investigative work wasn't generally her strong suit, but she'd had training in it. Just not as much as she'd had in hand-to-hand combat and weaponry. Which was why she wanted to have a look around his place in person and hope something would come to her, some clue as to why someone was so desperate to get him away from his home.

"I should drive," Cal said. "I don't want anything to happen to your car."

"Actually, I was thinking I should follow you over in my own car, then leave yours there. But I was also thinking we should make it look like I leave alone."

He nodded. "Smart. I can slip out the back and run to your house in a couple of minutes."

She folded the note back up and stuck it in her pocket. "Let me go tell Luis we're leaving and I'm good to go."

They got to Cal's house about ten minutes later. It was a beautiful place and similar in style to Everleigh Manor, but then a lot of the coastal homes had a similar New England feel. Lots of decks and big windows to take advantage of the stunning views. Most of the homes were two stories, as well, and stretched long and thin along the width of the property, again to make the most of the incredible views.

Front yards were deep once you got down the long drives that kept the homes from prying eyes.

Cal's home was accented with lots of stone and wood in the Arts and Crafts style. Ivy crept up one side of the manor and around part of the enormous front door. An arched stained-glass window above the door depicted a traditional three-pointed Celtic knot in shades of green and gold. It was lovely and charming, and she couldn't wait to see the inside.

Bess got out of her car, gaze sweeping the property for signs of danger or anything that didn't belong. It didn't take long to find something. Between the detached garage and the end of the house, a piece of heavy machinery was visible. Some kind of earth mover or something.

She tipped her head at it while she walked to where Cal was standing. "What's going on back there?"

He turned to look. "The old gazebo's about to get pulled down. It's in terrible shape, and I want a bigger one that's more useful."

"How old is it?"

He thought a moment. "Maybe eight or nine years? Whenever Jamie was here. He built it as a thank-you for letting him stay here, and it was nice of him, but he didn't use the right kind of wood, and the salt air just destroyed it."

She nodded, storing that info away. "Where were you when you got shot at?"

"Almost here," he answered, pointing to a tree at the edge of the drive. "That's where I found the bullet. Second time I was near the end of the drive, getting the mail. Never found that bullet."

She searched the surrounding woods, looking and listening for anything. "We should get inside before it happens a third time."

"Right." He led her down the flagstone path that went from the drive to the front door.

"Your house is beautiful. And feels like the design's been influenced by your home country, unless I'm wrong."

He smiled as he opened the door. "You're not." He stepped back to let her go in first. "Welcome to Ard na Mara, which roughly translates to house on a hill by the sea."

She stepped inside. For a house almost as large as hers, it felt like a cottage. Much cozier and lived in. Less like a museum. More like a home. The stone floors, exposed wood beams, and plastered walls added to that effect, but there was more to it than that. This house was lived in. And well loved.

Everleigh had never been anyone's home for more than a couple of months. "It's really lovely."

"Thank you." He closed the door behind him. "You want the tour, or should we just get straight to business?"

Curiosity got the best of her. "Let's split the difference. Quick tour."

He laughed. "Follow me."

The tour was fast, but it gave her plenty of time to see just how beautiful his home was. She didn't see anything unusual either, nothing that she interpreted as a clue. Plenty of valuables, though. Could that be why someone wanted Cal out? So they could loot the place?

Anything was possible, she supposed.

They ended up in the kitchen, which seemed to

be the heart of every home anyway, and Bess was surprised at how colorful it was. Bright blue tumbled tiles paved the floor, and butter-yellow cabinets lined the walls, all of it brought together with white marble countertops and a delft tile back-splash. On paper, she would have said it was too much. But standing in the middle of it was a different story. The views out the windows were very close to her own, but the similarities between the two kitchens ended there.

She glanced at him. "Did you pick all of this out?"

He snorted. "Not bloody likely. No, this is my ma's doing years ago. I should probably redo it, I guess."

"No." Bess shook her head. "You should leave it alone. It's really nice."

"Yeah?" He looked pleased with her assessment. "I'll go grab those letters."

"Bring the bullet too, if you still have it."

"All right." He returned a few minutes later and put the letters and the bullet on the counter.

She picked up the bullet first. "It's silver all right, but it's also small caliber—.22, looks like." She rolled it in her fingers. "This was never going to kill you. It wouldn't even make it all the way through you."

She set it back on the counter. "That shot and probably the second one were meant to scare you."

"I guess that's reassuring."

She pulled the note out of her pocket and laid it next to the letters. "It tells us something about whoever's behind this. They really do just want to scare you off."

He went over to the wall and flipped a switch, turning on a few more lights. "Handwriting looks the same to me."

"Me, too. Same paper as well. There's something odd about this paper, though. The size of it. You don't see perfectly square sheets of paper very often." She looked closer at the edges. "It's been cut down from a standard size. Maybe because it had a letterhead on it."

"Figuring out what that letterhead said is going to be impossible."

"Pretty close, but that's all right. It's still a clue. Business stationery isn't as common as it used to be. Lots of places do everything electronically."

"I suppose." He sighed, obviously frustrated. "What now?"

"I'd like to have a look around outside. You should pack a few things while I do that. Could be a few days until I get this sorted out."

"Right." But he was still frowning.

"Hey, I will figure this out. And while I'm doing that, you and Murphy are going to be safe at Everleigh. I realize it's not the same as being in your own home, but it won't be that bad."

He smiled. "The company is grand."

She laughed. "You'd better get some of Murphy's stuff too."

"I will. He'll be missin' his catnip mice for sure."

"What's the best door to use to get outside? I don't want to use the front one."

"You could go out onto one of the decks. Or through the main garage."

"Garage." She gestured behind her. "That way, right?"

"I'll show you." He started walking. "The house is a warren of rooms. You'll be lost in the map room before you know it. And this way I can give you a slightly more complete tour."

She followed. "You have a map room?"

"One of my uncles was an amateur cartographer."

Like that explained having an entire room dedicated to maps. But as they passed by and he pointed that room out, she stuck her head in to have a look. Maps of all shapes and sizes filled the space, including a gigantic three-paneled version of Ireland that covered most of one wall.

Globes of all kinds decorated a lot of the room as well. Some of them were amazingly intricate. "Okay, this is a lot cooler than I thought it would be. I mean, maps are interesting, but these are way more than that."

Cal grinned. "You want to see something really amazing?"

Without waiting for her response, he stepped into the room and flipped a switch. A spotlight turned on, illuminating a large glass-topped display table. "Come look."

Spurred on by the excitement in his voice alone, she did just that, joining him at the table's edge. "What is it? Besides a map, I mean."

"One of my great uncle's prize possessions. A Ptolemy atlas. Extremely rare. And extremely valuable."

"I can imagine." She tipped her head to see him better. "Valuable enough that someone would want you out of the house to get access to it?"

He stared at the atlas, finally shaking his head. "I don't think so. Not with everything else in this house. But maybe ..." He looked at her. "Maybe they want to nick all the McCarthy valuables."

"I thought about that. It's a possibility. But why your place? Dark Harbor Road is lousy with houses filled with pricey goods. There has to be something specific they'd be after."

Cal stiffened suddenly. "Franco Marr. He wants Moira's gin recipe."

CHAPTER

TEN

Bess frowned. "You mean that recipe is here in this house?"

Cal hesitated before answering, like he realized he'd let something slip. "Yes. But I must swear you to secrecy on that."

"I won't tell a soul. But you have it locked up, right? In a safe or a vault somewhere?"

More hesitation.

She rolled her eyes. "Let me guess. It's just hidden in a place that you're sure no one would ever think to look." She wasn't sure if that was genius or stupid. Probably a little of both. But she was leaning toward not genius.

He glanced away for a moment. "Look, no one knows it's here."

"Seems like *someone* knows it's here. Which means they might also know where it is. Or they at least have an idea."

"No one will ever find it." His gaze strayed away again.

The poor fool. She bit the inside of her cheek to

keep from laughing. "It's in this room, isn't it?"

The tiniest twitch of his brows answered that question. "Absolutely not. What would make you think that?"

"I bet I can come within ten feet of it."

"It's not in this room," he repeated.

She walked toward the bookshelf he'd glanced at earlier. "How am I doing?"

He frowned. "It's not over there."

Which meant it was. She put her hand on the highest shelf, about where he'd looked. A row of old-fashioned encyclopedias filled the shelf. She studied them. "I'd say it's either in *A* for alcohol, *G* for gin, *R* for recipe, or *S* for spirits. Is that close enough for you?"

He looked downright pouty now. "What kind of creature are you? Some sort of devil?"

She let out the laugh she'd held back a few moments ago. "Actually, no. I'm a descendant of the Nephilim."

"You have fallen angel blood in you." He inhaled audibly. "That explains so much."

"Like why you find my smell irresistible and why you thought I tasted like honey? Yes. But I promise, I'm not a mind reader. Just very observant and highly intuitive."

"So you've proven. But shouldn't you be out, I don't know, damning men's souls for eternity?"

Chuckling again, she walked back to him. "The line goes through the women in my family, and no, that's not what we do. Many generations ago, one of my ancestors took a vow to fight against our nature and do good on this earth. No one that came after her broke that vow, and so we continue to fight against the darkness."

He narrowed his eyes. "And ARROW had the gall to fire you? Do they know all of that?"

"They do. Many of my family have worked under their mantle." Although until he'd mentioned it, she'd forgotten about being fired for a while. She was too busy solving his problems. It felt good.

His gaze softened with empathy. "They don't deserve you."

She smiled, touched by his concern. "Thanks. I should really get outside and have that look around. And while I'm gone, you need to put that recipe in a safe. You do have a safe, right?"

"I do."

"Good. Garage?"

He showed her to it, then left her to do as she'd asked. There were two other cars in the garage. A Range Rover and an Aston Martin convertible. Navy blue and metallic gray. Both very nice. On a hunch, she checked the wheel wells on both of them and found two more trackers.

Things were starting to come together in her mind, but not enough that she was ready to make more than a guess about who was behind all of this. She still needed to see if there were any more clues to gather.

She left the trackers on the top step leading into the house, then slipped out the back door to have a look around. She hadn't bothered with a flashlight again. Much like at her house, Cal had landscape lighting, and that was sufficient.

With no real destination in mind, she wandered over to the gazebo, curious about the work being done. Exactly as Cal had said, the whole thing was in terrible shape. Everywhere she looked there was peeling paint, rotted wood, and rusted nails. It even seemed to be leaning slightly. He was right to take it down.

Would that bother his cousin? Jamie had built it, after all. Bess couldn't imagine that replacing the old gazebo with one that was structurally sound would be enough to upset someone. Not to the point of threats and violence. Or wanting to get Cal out of the house. That made no sense.

Also, this was Cal's property. He had the right to tear the thing down entirely and level the earth if he so desired.

But she still stood there, staring at it. Feeling like there was something she was missing. What was it? Maybe she needed to have a better look.

Reluctantly, she turned on her cell phone flashlight. She didn't like using the light because it made her a visible target in all of this darkness, but she needed to cross the gazebo off her list of possible clues once and for all.

With great caution, she went up the steps to examine the inside. She tested each spot before putting her full weight down. The first board creaked but held strong. She brought her other foot up but put it on a different board.

She turned her phone toward the ceiling. Small black pods hung from the rafters. Pods? Too late, she realized they were bats. They came swooping down toward her. She dropped to a crouch, not particularly afraid but not wanting one stuck in her hair or scratching her face.

As they flew off, she stood, checking the ceiling for more. In doing so, she shifted her stance onto an untested board.

Her foot went straight through, pitching her

forward. She held onto her phone as she fell. More boards cracked underneath her. She lay still for a moment, doing a quick mental once-over. Other than a few scrapes, she didn't feel injured.

What she did feel was that scum of some variety covered the remaining floorboards. She didn't want to think too much about what that might be.

Mostly, her pride was a little wounded. Stepping without thinking had been a dumb move. She blamed the bats for the distraction. But she again agreed that Cal was right to tear this thing down. It was a hazard.

She carefully freed her foot from the splintered wood. Her jeans were torn. She stayed on her butt and scooted back toward the steps. Her phone bounced light all around the interior as she moved. Once she got onto firmer ground, she took another look around.

Nothing she saw—not the ceiling (now bat-free), not the support columns, and not the short side walls—held anything that looked vaguely clue-like. She shined the light into the hole her foot had made. Nothing down there either but bare, undulating dirt.

So much for that theory.

She got to her feet. A sharp pain radiated down one shin. She tipped the light toward herself.

Through the rip that ran from knee to ankle, blood was visible on her shin.

That wasn't going to instill confidence in Cal that she was able to take care of herself, was it? Frustrated, she sighed. She could heal just as well as he could, but that only worked on skin, not jeans. There was no way to hide what had happened.

She was about to head down the stairs and continue her walk around the house when the snap of a branch some ways off made her go still again.

Was she being watched? She listened more intently, filtering out the ambient sounds to focus deeply on what else might be out there. Try as she might, she didn't pick up the heartbeat she'd expected to.

She inhaled, trying to find another way to identify her possible watcher, but the wind was going in the wrong direction.

Regardless, the small hairs on the back of her neck were all the convincing she needed. Someone was out there.

Suddenly, she changed her mind about Cal staying at her house. He needed to be here, at his own house, where whoever was after him was most likely to try something again.

Which meant she needed to be here, too.

CHAPTER

ELEVEN

"As much as I don't want to leave you alone, I also don't want to give whoever's after you an opportunity to get into the house while it's empty. If that happens and he gets what he wants, we've lost the chance to grab him."

Cal stood there, looking like he was listening, but Bess wasn't entirely sure. He'd been fixated on her injured leg since she returned. Probably not such an odd thing, considering the sight and smell of blood were his main weaknesses. "That seems like a pretty serious injury. Are you positive we shouldn't clean it? What if that scratch came from a rusty nail?"

"I'm up to date on my shots. And while I might not be a vampire, I can assure you that I heal with the same efficiency. I'll clean myself up when I get back to my house. I have to change anyway."

He sighed. "I still think I should go with you. After all, someone has to deal with Murphy. Putting him in his carrier is only easy if he thinks it's *his* idea. And, I might also point out, I have been away from the house for some time today and there are no signs that anyone was here."

"Because they were busy throwing a brick through my window." But there was no evidence that anyone had tried to get in either. She'd walked the perimeter before coming back inside so that she could check all the doors and operable windows. Not a single one appeared to have been tampered with. There weren't even any scratch marks by the locks.

She relented. She had better things to do than argue with him anyway. "Fine. But only because of Murphy. It's going to be a quick trip. I'm going to change, throw some clothes in a bag, grab my chargers, and that's it. Fifteen minutes, tops."

"Fine with me." He was smiling. Of course.

"All right, I get it. You think you won."

He laughed. "This is not a competition. But we're safer together. And this way you can keep an eye on me."

"True." She didn't know about the safer together bit. "But set your security alarm when we leave. Just in case someone does try to break in."

"About that ... I don't have a security alarm."

She stared at him. "In *this* house you don't have an alarm."

He smiled like that was amusing. "Nope."

He was having way too much fun with this. She shook her head. "At the very least, you really should get some staff that live on property like I have."

He shrugged. "I had a groundskeeper once years ago, but he up and left without a word. Doesn't matter. I'm here all the time. I have people that come in on a regular basis. But it's different when you're a vampire. Hiring is harder. You have to be sure you're getting some kind of supernaturals, too, so that they understand. And you can't exactly advertise for that."

"There are companies that specialize in help for supernatural employers." She knew because she'd once raided the offices of a firm like that. Staffing hadn't been the problem. The issue had been the human trafficking operation they'd been a cover for.

He nodded. "I know. You're right. I should hire some live-ins. But ..." He made a face.

"You like your privacy. I get it."

"I do. You do too."

"No argument there." They were a lot alike in ways. She'd never imagined that would be true about her and a vampire. "All right, let's get this done."

When they got to her house, she went straight to her bedroom to change and pack a bag while Cal went off to find Murphy.

But Bess found him first. The furry beast was asleep on her bed again. She laughed as she stuck her head out the door. "Cal, he's in here again."

A second later, Cal materialized next to her, carrier in hand. "Such a traitor himself is."

"Mother of pearl." She jerked back as she sucked in a ragged breath, caught off guard by his speed. "Don't do that."

"Sorry," he said. "Did I startle you?"

She wasn't about to admit to that. "I just wasn't expecting you to show up so suddenly."

His eyes narrowed. "Can't you move that fast?"

She didn't quite have *that* kind of speed. "I have skills. I just don't use them as much as you. ARROW drilled it into us to appear human as often as possible."

"Makes sense if you're trying to fly under the radar. Well, you don't have to be shy about your abilities around me."

"Good to know."

He tipped his head toward Murphy. "May I?"

She stepped out of the doorway. "Do you need me to help?"

"Might not be a bad idea in case he decides to do a runner." He glanced back at the door. "In fact, might be best not to leave any escape routes."

She shut the bedroom door, keenly aware that she was now closed in her bedroom with the sexiest vampire she'd ever known. "What should I do?"

"Try not to laugh." Cal rolled his eyes. "He likes it when I sing to him. At least it distracts him enough that he ignores the fact that I'm putting him in the carrier."

Bess snorted. "All righty then." The very thought of Cal singing to his cat had started something inside her that felt very much like the giggles.

He opened his mouth and began. *"Too-ra-loo-ra-loo-ral, Too-ra-loo-ra-li …"*

His voice was surprisingly sweet. She could see why Murphy liked it.

The cat rolled over onto his back, practically smiling at Cal. Cal kept up the singing as he lifted Murphy and slipped him into the carrier. He stopped singing the moment the latch was shut. "Good boyo, Murph." Then he looked at Bess. "Thank you for not laughing."

"You have a nice voice."

"Thanks." He picked up the carrier, but his gaze went to her torn jeans again. "I'll give you your privacy."

She opened the bedroom door to let him out. "Couple of minutes."

"Take your time."

He left, and she closed the door again. He cooked and cleaned, he sang to his cat, and he kissed like nobody's business. Why did she feel like she was in trouble?

Didn't matter. She'd solve his problem, and then she'd never have to see him again. Unless she wanted to.

She groaned. Enough already. She got a bag packed, then stripped her clothes off so she could clean the blood from her leg with a damp washcloth. Underneath the blood and dirt, there wasn't a mark left. "Take that, Cal."

She changed into thick black leggings, a long-sleeved thermal T-shirt, and her combat boots. He knew what she used to do. There was no reason to look any differently now. Although she didn't bother adding any blades. It was clear that Cal was not a threat.

She grabbed her bag and met him back out in the kitchen. He was on the phone, so she busied herself with cleaning out the coffee maker while she waited.

"Not yet, no," he said. "I'm not sure. Up to the demolition company at this point. Just waiting on them. All right. You too. Bye."

He hung up. "Sorry. Jamie called to chat. He does that sometimes when he's traveling. You ready?"

She put the carafe back in the machine. "Yep."

On the ride back, she asked him about Franco Marr. "What else can you tell me about this guy?"

"His family has been in competition with mine for a long time. Big rivalry. All started when we introduced a honey whiskey at the same time they did. Problem was, ours launched two weeks after theirs. They swore we were copying them."

She hooked her hand under the shoulder belt as she turned to look at him a little more. "Were you?"

Cal frowned. "Not a chance. You know how long it takes to develop a thing like that? A long time. If we were really copying them, it would have been a year before we'd have product on the shelf. They knew that, but it was good for their business to make a fuss about it."

"Made them seem like the victim."

"Right. And got them all kinds of publicity where Franco was happy to be quoted as saying they'd done it first."

"I see. How did you handle it?"

"We put out a statement outlining how long our whiskey had been in development, offered tours of our production facilities, and began a promotion where we gave pubs free bottles to do their own taste comparisons with." Cal grinned, eyes still on the road. "All the hullabaloo went away pretty quick after that."

Bess smiled. "That was good thinking. I could see how he'd love to get ahold of your gin recipe. It would be quite a coup for him to launch a product that was a duplicate of yours."

"I'm sure he'd do it at a lower price, too. Anything to undercut us."

Cal turned into his drive, and Murphy let out a meow. "That's right. We're home."

Bess glanced back at Murphy. The cat had been quiet the whole time until now. Could he really sense they were home? "He's a beautiful cat with a great personality."

"That he is," Cal agreed.

"Do you think Franco Marr is at his house? I mean, could it actually be him that's been bothering you? Or do you think he'd hire that out?"

Cal turned off the car. "I don't know. He hates me enough that he'd probably want to do it himself. He thinks he's smart enough not to get caught, too."

"That's the fae in him," she said.

"No doubt. Why? You want to drive past his place? See if the lights are on?"

She shook her head. "No. I'll do it myself. And I don't plan to drive."

CHAPTER
TWELVE

B ess dropped her bag in the guest room Cal had shown her to, then, while he went to feed Murphy, she stepped out onto the deck. Much like Everleigh Manor, Ard na Mara had decks all along the back so the views could be enjoyed from every room.

The temperature had dropped again, and there seemed to be the promise of snow in the air, but the wind had died down a bit, meaning there was no better time to do what she needed to do.

She took a few steps toward the railing, shifting forms as she moved. She landed on the railing with a little hop and a strong flap of her wings. She'd taken on the goshawk again. It was a strong bird with keen eyesight and few enemies.

She glanced back at the glass doors she'd just come through, catching her reflection. Then she launched skyward, getting some airtime to acclimate herself to having wings. After a moment of that, she headed for Marr's house. She'd mapped it out online, knew his house number, and had the route in her head.

A quick circle and she dove down toward the street. It was much easier to follow the road than the coast. While watching for branches and cars, she counted off houses as she flew.

She slowed as she approached Marr's house, landing on the mailbox. This was the house. Lights were on, but that didn't mean anything. Could be staff or timers designed to make the house look lived in. She needed to see if there were actually people in there. Namely Marr. She'd found a few pictures of him online so that she could recognize him.

A few flaps of her wings and she was coasting toward the front porch. She banked and went up over the house to land on the back deck. More lights. And this time, people.

Franco Marr and a slightly younger woman. His wife maybe? Or girlfriend? Bess wasn't sure, but Franco was definitely at home. She tipped her head, trying to overhear them, but the football game was on, making it hard to hear much else.

They weren't talking anyway. The woman was on her phone, and Franco was engaged in the game, reacting to the action on the screen with a few shouts and groans.

Nothing about him looked like a man who might be actively trying to threaten Cal out of his house. Franco was balding, paunchy, and had the pallor of a man whose biggest outside activity was getting packages off the front porch. This wasn't a guy who was camping out in the woods around Cal's house, waiting for him to show.

Still, he had the look of a man who thought he was big stuff. A definite air of self-importance. Typical fae.

If he was the one behind Cal's threats, she'd bet Everleigh Manor that he'd hired the work out.

She hopped off the railing and up onto a nearby plant stand full of mums gone to seed. Could the woman be behind it? She didn't exactly look like the sharpest tool in the shed, but looks could be deceiving.

Franco's attention shifted suddenly to something beyond the television. He patted the arm of the recliner he was sitting in, smiling and calling out to whatever he was looking at. Another person?

A fluffy gray Persian jumped up onto his lap.

Bess would have smiled if she'd been able. Franco was a cat guy too? Was that because Cal had a cat? Interesting.

He scratched the cat's head and seemed to be

talking baby talk to it. He clearly adored the little animal. It got her thinking. A plan began to form.

Cal might not like it, but there'd be no real danger. Not to him or Murphy. Just to Bess. And danger was just a day's work for her.

Lost in thought, she suddenly became aware that the cat on Franco's lap was staring at her through the glass.

Without hesitation, she took to the air. She'd seen enough. Franco Marr was indeed at his house, which meant he could be the guy behind the threats to Cal. Especially if he wanted to personally get his hand on that gin recipe.

All she had to do now was find a way to lure him into a trap and prove it.

She landed on Cal's deck a few minutes later, right outside the living room. Cal was standing at the door, Murphy in his arms. Maybe waiting on her?

She took human form again and approached.

As she did, he saw her and opened the door. "Did you see him?"

"I did. He's there. There's a woman with him. Maybe his wife?"

"Could be Mary Lou, his third wife." Cal stepped

back to let her in. "And if he's home, then he could be doing all of this."

"Absolutely." She reached up to pet Murphy, but a gust of air howled through the house just then, spooking the cat.

He jumped out of Cal's arms and zipped through the door.

Cal let out a soft groan. "Not again."

"Come on," Bess said. "We'll grab him before he goes too far."

They headed out after Murphy. The cat was trotting toward the far end of the deck. Toward the woods.

"Can you believe that?" Cal said. "I think he's going to your house again."

"Maybe he likes my brand of tuna."

Cal laughed. "Maybe."

Perhaps sensing he was being followed, Murphy picked up speed and zoomed down the deck steps and went straight for the gazebo.

She and Cal picked up speed as well, reaching the gazebo just in time to see Murphy disappear into the hole made by Bess falling through the floor.

Then she heard a sound that set all her nerve endings on alert.

Cal opened his mouth to say something, but Bess clamped her hand over it, giving him a look as she put her finger to her ear.

He frowned but nodded in understanding.

Softly, from the other side of the gazebo, the sound filtered through again.

"*Psp psp psp.*"

She took her hand off Cal's mouth to grab his sleeve and tug him down into a crouch next to her. Then she put her mouth to his ear to whisper, "Someone's trying to call Murphy."

As the sound registered, Cal's face turned into a mask of anger.

She understood. But the idea that had come to her earlier finally hatched. "Listen to me." She quickly mapped out her plan, keeping her voice low and whispering directly into his ear.

When she finished, Cal was still frowning. "I don't like it."

"I don't care."

He rolled his eyes but sighed. Bess took that as his agreement. "Fine. But I still need to get Murphy out of there."

"Right."

Cal stood up and, in a louder than necessary

voice, said, "Come on, boyo. That's enough exploring. Let's go. *Now.*"

Bess got to her feet as well. There was no denying the force of Cal's last word. He'd clearly laced it with persuasion, a skill only old vampires possessed.

She instantly appreciated that he hadn't used it on her. Although she was pretty sure she'd be able to resist.

As it seemed, however, Murphy couldn't. He popped up through the hole in the gazebo floor and meowed at Cal.

Bess grinned. Then she squinted at Cal. "Why didn't you just do that earlier at my house?"

Cal shrugged innocently, like the idea had never occurred to him. "Guess I just forgot."

Or maybe he'd wanted a reason to stay connected to Bess. If that was true, it was a little flattering, to be honest.

Cal patted his leg. "Come on. Get over here, you naughty thing."

Murphy trotted over, meowing again. A strand of cobweb clung to one ear.

Cal held out his arms, and Murphy jumped into them, rubbing his face against Cal's neck.

"That cat," Bess said.

"I know," Cal answered. "Let's get inside."

All three of them traipsed back up the steps and into the house through the kitchen entrance. Once inside, Cal gave Murphy a kiss on the head before setting him on the floor. "That's enough of the escaping now, you hear? Let's get you some biscuits."

He went over to a jar on the counter, fished out a few treats and tossed them to Murphy, who promptly inhaled them.

Cal leaned on the counter and looked at Bess. "You sure this is a smart idea?"

"You have a better one?"

He shook his head reluctantly. "No."

"I've set up stings more times than I can count," Bess said. "All I need for this to work is for the guy hiding in the woods out there to buy in. And there's no reason he won't if you play your part."

"How many of those stings went wrong?"

She tipped her head, amused by his concern. "None. I'm very good at what I do."

Grudging amusement lit his eyes. "So I've heard."

"That is why you wanted me to tackle this case in the first place, remember?"

"I do. I just didn't figure on … caring about you."

His admission threw her. She swallowed before answering. "I appreciate that. I feel the same."

She really did, too. As hard to admit as it was, she cared about a vampire. She lifted her chin slightly. "I promise I can handle what I'm about to do. This will all be wrapped up very soon."

"I believe you." He looked at the clock. "How long should we wait?"

"Not long. We don't want our guy getting restless and calling it a night. Maybe a few more minutes. Or maybe … now. Let's just do it."

For a moment, Cal said nothing. "Fine."

"Don't deviate from the script."

He gave her a look but kept his mouth shut. Was that his way of not promising to do as she'd asked? She wasn't sure, but she didn't want to get into it.

He turned and walked off through the house. She followed. Silence hung between them, a weighty blanket of tension that said more than words could. He was worried about her. And she was focused on the mission ahead.

They went into the garage, and he pushed the button to open one of the bays. The muted light of dawn was already beginning to brighten the shards of sky visible between the bare tree branches. The wind twisted a cluster of leaves into a little eddy on the driveway.

"Be safe," he said softly.

She nodded, giving him a little smile. "Promise."

Resigned, he grabbed a trash can and started to wheel it out.

Behind him, she shifted into a new form. Murphy's.

CHAPTER
THIRTEEN

I n cat form, she darted out of the garage.

Right on cue, Cal played his part. He dropped the garbage can and came after her. "Murphy! I told you to stay in the house!"

She scampered away, headed toward the gazebo again. She paused inches from the hole in the floor, waiting for Cal to catch up and do his last bit.

He stood in front of the steps, shaking his head in utter displeasure. "You naughty git. I'm not going in there after you. You want to rummage around under that dirty thing, you go ahead. You'll be crying to come in in no time."

Bess meowed at him for good effect.

Cal held his hands up. "You know where the door is." His voice was edged with frustration and annoyance.

Bess was smiling on the inside. Cal was a good actor.

He walked away, shaking his head and muttering about cats who didn't appreciate the good life indoors.

If she could have, she would have laughed.

A couple moments later, she heard the familiar *psp psp psp* again. She jumped through the hole in the floor so she was where she was supposed to be.

The space under the floor was dirt and rocks and debris that had accumulated over the years. At least it smelled like years of debris. Not only was there a salty dampness in the air but the funk of organic matter decomposing.

The piers holding up the gazebo looked to be in good shape, despite the cobwebs and other detritus strewn about under there, but it was easy to see how deteriorated the floorboards were. No wonder she'd fallen through.

The dirt had never been leveled either, apparently. Maybe it was too big a job when the gazebo had first been built, but she imagined Cal would want that fixed before the new gazebo went up. Especially because on the left side, it looked like a significant sinkhole was developing. If it got close enough to the piers, that whole side might collapse.

"*Psp psp psp.* Here, kitty kitty." Footsteps crunched through the underbrush on the far side, growing slowly closer.

She sat down to wait under the hole in the floor. She wouldn't make him work too hard. That wasn't the point. She wanted to be caught. Her whole plan hinged on it.

Her gaze returned to the sinkhole. Odd that it should occur like it had. Sort of long and narrow. Maybe five and a half feet. And very much shaped like a—a hand snatched her by the scruff of her neck and pulled her up out of the hole.

She hadn't expected Cal's stalker to act so decisively. How would Murphy react to being grabbed? Yowl? Go limp? Take a swipe at the guy?

Before she could decide on a response, she was face to face with her kidnapper, a man with bright green eyes, but that and his mouth were all she could see of his face. The rest was covered in a ski mask.

He smiled at her. "Hello there, Murph. Remember me? Been a while, eh? Can't have you running off again, now can we?"

The accent was faint, but it was definitely there. And definitely Irish. Coincidence that Franco Marr's hired thug came from the same place Cal did? Bess didn't think so. Not when the man was so familiar with Murphy.

He tucked her into the crook of his arm, caught her jaw between his fingers, pried it open, and tossed something down her throat. A pill.

She gagged, but the action only sent the pill

further down. She could feel it dissolving, coating her tongue in bitter grit. She swallowed involuntarily. He'd drugged her, obviously. Her only option was to shift out of this form immediately, even if that was earlier than planned.

But the shift wouldn't come. Had the drug already entered her system? Seemed like it. At this size and with her speedy metabolism, it was no wonder it had hit her so fast and hard.

She struggled to keep her eyes open even as everything she'd just seen and heard began to jell in her head. She completely understood what was going on, and she had a pretty good idea of who was behind it all and why.

She had to shift. Had to fight the fog drifting over her.

But try as she might, everything faded, and a moment later, all went dark.

Bess woke up, groggy and dazed and still very much in Murphy's form. How much later, she had no idea. She managed to get her eyes open to slits, but nothing around her looked familiar.

She was in a studio apartment. A small bank of cabinets against the far wall held a sink and a hot plate. Above the sink was a small window. The sky was brighter than it had been, but it didn't look like that much time had passed since they'd been at Cal's.

In front of the cabinets sat a man at a worn kitchen table, writing something. The acrid smell of Sharpie markers hung in the air, another sign that this was indeed Cal's stalker.

A wave of nausea hit her, and the urge to vomit rose in her throat. She closed her eyes again, letting the darkness soothe her while she tried to remember what had happened. The gazebo. The sinkhole. The man with the accent.

It all fell together.

She had to shift and deal with this guy. She opened her eyes a little more this time, staying still so as not to attract attention to herself. At least he hadn't put her in a cage. She seemed to be lying on the foot of the bed of a fold-out couch. The blanket was scratchy beneath her furred cheek.

The good news was that whatever he drugged her with felt like it was wearing off already. That was the blessing and the curse of her changeling metabolism. She processed things fast, which was why she'd fallen under the drug's sway so quickly and why she was now shedding its influence just as easily.

Another minute or two and she felt confident

that her ability to shift would be back. She used that time to further assess the space and her kidnapper. Years of experience said he was some kind of supernatural. She moved her head slightly to get a better view.

A bottle of McCarthy's Red Whiskey sat on the table. He folded the note he'd been writing, then picked up an envelope.

Time to shift. She couldn't wait any longer or she'd lose her advantage. But once again, her body would not obey her commands.

Her only recourse was to act in her current form, forcing her metabolism to speed up even further. She got to her four feet. A little wobbly but more in control than not. She crouched, then launched herself into the air. She landed on the stalker's shoulders, digging her claws in and raking them down his back as gravity pulled her to the floor.

He yowled and spun around, throwing her off to one side. She landed against the base of the cabinets with a hard thunk. He snarled and hissed, showing off fangs. *Vampire.* "I don't want to hurt you, Murphy, but if I have to—"

Her body obeyed this time, and she shifted into human form. She grabbed a knife from the block on the counter. "On the ground, vampire. Or I will run this through your heart and turn you into ash."

His eyes went wide, but before he could say anything, the door to the apartment burst open.

Cal stood there, fangs out, fire in his eyes, vibrating with anger. "Jamie. How could you?"

"I knew it," she muttered. Well, she hadn't known *for sure* her kidnapper was Cal's cousin, but she'd been leaning in that direction since the sinkhole and the accent.

Cal glanced at her. "You okay?"

"Fine." She nodded at his cousin. "But he's in a lot of trouble."

Cal nodded. "No kidding."

"I don't mean because he tried to kidnap your cat. I mean because of the body he's trying to keep you from finding under the gazebo."

Cal's eyes rounded, and Jamie deflated a bit, as if he knew he was defeated.

He let out a groan and shook his head, glaring at Bess. "You had to get involved."

Cal looked at his cousin. "Is she right? Did you bury someone under the gazebo? Is that why you built the thing in the first place?"

A muscle in Jamie's jaw twitched. "I never thought you'd tear it down."

"You shouldn't have built it with substandard lumber then." Cal shook his head. "Who is it? Who's under there?"

"Lenny Campbell."

Cal's jaw went south. "The gardener who went missing? Why on earth would you kill him?"

"I didn't mean to," Jamie started. His shoulders slumped forward. "I'd gone too long without feeding. I lost control." He repeated himself, softer this time. "I didn't mean to."

To Bess, it all made sense. "That's why you were trying to get Cal out of his house. So you could move the body?"

Jamie nodded. "Or at least make sure there wasn't anything to be found when they took the old gazebo down."

"I don't think there's much to be found." She kept the knife aimed at him. "There's a sinkhole where the body was, so that's a pretty sure sign it's decomposed."

Jamie shook his head. "Why did you have to get involved?"

"Because I asked her to," Cal said. "And because she found Murphy when he got out."

Jamie frowned. "I thought he'd come to me, but he ran off before I could grab him."

Cal's brows rose. "You let Murphy out?"

Jamie shrugged. "I just opened the door."

Bess glanced at Cal. "Does he have a key?"

Cal nodded. "You do, don't you Jamie?"

"Yes," his cousin answered. "And thankfully, you never changed the locks."

Cal looked at Bess. "I will be now."

She tipped her chin at Jamie. "What are you going to do with him?"

Cal's brow furrowed. "You're not going to turn him in to ARROW?"

"I don't work for them anymore." She also knew what Jamie's fate would be if she did that. A swift execution. And while he may have killed a man, she believed it was accidental. Still didn't justify drinking from the gardener. "But he should be locked up. A man is dead. And he could have seriously hurt you, too. He certainly made enough attempts."

Jamie took a step toward Cal. "I would never do any of that again. I swear it on my life."

Pain and sadness filled Cal's gaze. "You made some terrible decisions, Jamie. We have no choice but to turn you over to the authorities."

Jamie stared blankly at his cousin for a moment,

then his face twisted up in a snarl. "I am *not* going to jail."

"Yes, you are," Bess said.

He turned and lunged toward her with almost untrackable speed.

Instinct kicked in. The blade came up.

Jamie gasped. His eyes widened. And then he went to ash.

CHAPTER

FOURTEEN

Flakes of gray soot drifted down like snow.

Bess swallowed and looked at Cal. "I didn't mean to—"

His gaze was on the ash accumulating on the floor. "You did what you had to do. He would have hurt you."

She nodded slowly. "I'm still sorry. He was your family."

Cal came toward her, circling around the ash, and took her in his arms. He kept her there for a moment, but it felt like he was the one who needed comforting. "It's over."

She nodded, letting him hold her. He had to be grieving.

Finally, he pushed her away but held her shoulders, looking her over. "Are you sure you're all right? What happened?"

"As soon as he grabbed me, he gave me a pill, some kind of sedative. It hit me fast and hard. I passed out. How did you find me?"

He smiled. "I followed you." Then the smile went away. "I didn't know it was Jamie though."

"He had a ski mask on."

"Yes. Thankfully, he didn't take you far. This is the caretaker's cottage of the house next door. No idea where the caretaker is. I hope he's not another of Jamie's victims."

"I hope not too. Maybe they just don't have a caretaker at the moment." She glanced at the ash. "If it's okay with you, I'd like to get out of here."

"Me, too. I'm so glad you're okay. I can't believe it was Jamie. I can't believe he killed Lenny." Cal let out a weighty sigh. "This wasn't at all what I expected."

He still looked sad, and her heart hurt for him. She couldn't imagine the loss and betrayal he was feeling. Getting made redundant was nothing compared to this. "I'm really sorry."

He let go of her, and his smile returned, briefly. "Don't be. I owe you for figuring this out."

She touched his arm. "Just doing what you hired me to do."

He took her hand. "I don't know about you, but I could use a shower and some sleep. I may not have the same issues with the sun as other vampires, but that doesn't mean I enjoy being awake during daylight hours."

She probably had ash in her hair. She squeezed his hand as she answered. "A shower and sleep sound great."

He started for the door. "You can stay at my place, you know. If you want. That guest room is all yours."

"Good," she answered. "Because it's been a long night, and I'm ready to crash. I could probably make it back to my house, but that feels like a lot of work right now."

Fortunately, getting back to his house just meant a long walk through the wooded property that connected his neighbor's place with his.

They went in through the front door, which was still unlocked, but she noticed Cal turned the deadbolt when he shut it behind her.

"Sleep well."

"Thanks," she said. "You too. If I'm not here when you get up ..."

He paused, like he was searching for words. "I understand. But I hope that's not the case."

She just answered with a quick smile, then went in the direction of the guest room.

The shower was big, the water pressure perfect, and the toiletries luxurious. She washed everything, including her hair, then wrapped herself in towels that felt as deep and thick as a New England fog.

The blinds were already drawn to keep out the daylight, so the room was blissfully dark. She climbed into the bed, which seemed to have a mattress made out of clouds, and instantly felt the pull of sleep.

She'd get a couple of hours, then gather her things and go back to her own place. She and Cal could settle up some other time. She wasn't worried about that.

No longer able to keep her eyes open, she gave in and went to sleep.

When she opened her eyes again, it took a moment to remember where she was. She'd slept hard. For how long, she wasn't sure. Didn't feel like long.

She rolled over, stretched a little while still lying down, and thought about going back to sleep. The bed was deeply comfortable. But she wasn't really sleepy anymore.

Instead she got up and checked her phone. It was only eleven. What time had it been when they'd returned to Cal's house? Maybe seven? Or close to it.

She pulled on her clothes, packed up her few

things, then made her bed and left the guest room behind.

It was dark in the house, but then she imagined a vampire's house would be, because like Cal had implied, being immune to the sun didn't mean he was interested in embracing it.

She smelled coffee as she got closer to the kitchen. Was he up too? She found that hard to believe, but the aroma was impossible to ignore.

She dropped her bag by the door and wandered into the kitchen to investigate.

Cal stood at the French doors in the dining area, coffee in hand. The world beyond was dark.

Dark?

"Evening," he said.

She frowned. "Evening? What time is it?"

He looked over, glancing at the wall clock before answering her. "Five past eleven."

"At night?" She put a hand to her forehead. "Wow. I really slept. I thought it was eleven in the morning."

He laughed softly. "Sorry, no." Then he gestured with his cup. "Have some coffee."

"Thanks." She went toward the machine to help herself. "I didn't mean to stay this long."

"What's the rush to get home?"

She filled the mug he'd left out for her and

shrugged. "I need to figure out what I'm doing with the rest of my life, for one thing."

When she looked up from adding sugar, he was smiling at her. "You could always work for me."

She let out a little chuckle. "Doing what?"

"I have lousy security."

That made her laugh harder. "You really do." Then she looked at him again. "Are you being serious?" He couldn't be.

He walked closer to lean against the counter beside her. "Absolutely. I need the help. You said yourself I should hire some."

"I didn't mean me."

"But why not?"

Yeah, why not? He was nothing like any vampire she'd ever met. Of course, most of the vampires she'd met had been on murderous rampages. But Cal was sweet and kind and handsome and genuine.

And she liked him more than she would have thought possible. Working for him wouldn't be a hardship. "I'd need to know what your interpersonal relationship polices are."

He blinked. "My what?"

"Do you frown on employee-employer fraternization?"

He blinked again, then a big grin spread across his face. "It's encouraged, actually."

A little thrill went down her spine. "I really do need a job, especially if I'm going to have two little black cats to keep in treats and nip."

His eyes sparkled. "You're going to adopt Chip and Dip?"

She nodded. "And then immediately change their names."

"Does that mean you accept my offer?"

She traced a finger down his chest. "Well, I don't really know what that offer is yet …"

"It's whatever it takes to keep you around."

"Then I accept."

He pulled her into his arms and kissed her on the mouth, the taste of coffee sweet on his lips. "Grand."

She smiled up at him. "Somehow I knew you'd say that."

Want to be up to date on new books, audiobooks, and other fun stuff from me? Sign-up for my newsletter on my website, www.kristenpainter.com. No spam, just news (sales, freebies, releases, you know all that jazz.)

If you loved the book and want to see the series grow, tell a friends about the book and take time to leave a review!

Lost in Las Vegas: A Frost And Crowe Mystery

HappilyEverlasting Series:

Witchful Thinking

PARANORMAL ROMANCE

Nocturne Falls Series:

The Vampire's Mail Order Bride

The Werewolf Meets His Match

The Gargoyle Gets His Girl

The Professor Woos The Witch

The Witch's Halloween Hero – short story

The Werewolf's Christmas Wish – short story

The Vampire's Fake Fiancée

The Vampire's Valentine Surprise – short story

The Shifter Romances The Writer

The Vampire's True Love Trials – short story

The Vampire's Accidental Wife

The Reaper Rescues The Genie

The Detective Wins The Witch

The Vampire's Priceless Treasure

The Werewolf Dates The Deputy

The Siren Saves The Billionaire

Shadowvale Series:

The Trouble With Witches

The Vampire's Cursed Kiss

The Forgettable Miss French

Moody And The Beast

Her First Taste Of Fire

Sin City Collectors Series

Queen Of Hearts

Dead Man's Hand

Double or Nothing

Standalone Paranormal Romance:

Dark Kiss of the Reaper

Heart of Fire

Recipe for Magic

Miss Bramble and the Leviathan

All Fired Up

URBAN FANTASY

The House of Comarré series:

Forbidden Blood

Blood Rights

Flesh and Blood

Bad Blood

Out For Blood

Last Blood

The Crescent City series:

House of the Rising Sun

City of Eternal Night

Garden of Dreams and Desires

Nothing is completed without an amazing team.

Many thanks to:

Editor: Chris Kridler
Interior Formating: Gem Promotions

ABOUT THE AUTHOR

USA Today Best Selling Author Kristen Painter is a little obsessed with cats, books, chocolate, and shoes. It's a healthy mix. She loves to entertain her readers with interesting twists and unforgettable characters. She currently writes the best-selling paranormal romance series, Nocturne Falls, and award-winning urban fantasy. The former college English teacher can often be found all over social media where she loves to interact with readers.

For more information go to
www.kristenpainter.com

For More Paranormal Women's Fiction Visit:
www.paranormalwomensfiction.net

Made in United States
North Haven, CT
11 March 2022

17007151R00078